2047

Short Stories from Our Common Future

Edited by Tanja Rohini Bisgaard

By
Tanja Rohini Bisgaard
Kimberly Christensen
Richard Friedman
John A. Frochio
Julie Gram
Alison Halderman
Lene K. Kristoffersen
Ruth Mundy
L X Nishimoto
Isaac Yuen
David Zetland

2047: Short stories from Our Common Future

Contents

Acknowledgments

We would like to thank everyone who contributed to making this anthology possible. In particular, everyone who supported us via the crowdfunding site Indiegogo so we could raise funds to hire a professional copy editor.

Thank you to:

Ahmed Mansour
Alexandra Almasi
Anna Constant
Brian Gonzalez
Bruce Herrmann
Claus Gladyszak
Emil Damgaard Grann
Hanne Juel
Hugh and Melissa Mundy
Ingrid Wawra
Jacob Kornum
Karina Ransby
Lis Poulsen
Maggie Rose
Mark Jenkins
Michael Moncur
Morten Blaauw
Nathaniel Herrmann
Nils Bisgaard
Rosemary Christensen
Ryan Mizzen

Siril Kleiven
Søren Femmer Jensen
Steinar Valade-Amland
Stèphane Pisani
Susanne Bisgaard

(Some of the individuals who donated have chosen to remain anonymous, so their names do not appear on this list.)

Finally, we would like to thank Angela Brown for helping us make our stories the best they can be, and Kristian Bjornard for the cover design.

Introduction

As a teenager in the 1980s, growing up in Norway's second-largest city, Bergen, I often sat reading the newspaper before heading off to school. What made the greatest impression on me, and stayed with me for years, was the news about acid rain damaging forests in Europe, and radiation from Chernobyl being found in reindeer lichen in northern Norway. These were problems that seemed local to those experiencing them, yet these problems could only be solved by every nation working together globally.

This year, 2017, marks the thirtieth anniversary of the Brundtland Commission's presentation of its work, led by Norway's former prime minister, Gro Harlem Brundtland. The General Assembly of the United Nations appointed the commission to create a vision for a sustainable future. The definition of "sustainability" found in the report *Our Common Future* is still used today by academics, the business community as well as the civil society:

"Sustainable development is development that meets the needs of the present without compromising the ability of future generations to meet their own needs."

A great amount of progress occurred very quickly in some areas, while it's taken longer for action to be implemented in others. A global agreement on reducing the impacts of climate change wasn't reached until 2015. Politicians, however, are now putting green growth on their national agendas. Companies are innovating to produce without polluting and are using fewer resources. Nongovernmental organizations (NGOs) continue to create awareness of climate and environmental problems that must be solved. And more and more citizens are making conscious choices regarding how to live sustainably.

Still, I often wonder: what will the world look like in another thirty years if global warming and environmental degradation aren't reduced as much as we hope? And how will we deal with those problems? After all, no matter which models scientists are using today, it's impossible to accurately forecast what will happen.

So I gathered a group of authors and asked them to write their vision of what the world will look like in 2047. We want our short stories to make you reflect, or provoke you, or bring feelings to the surface while you read them. And hopefully all of them will make you realize that your actions matter and will encourage you to take part in caring for the world and the people in it.

I hope we will succeed in having an effect on you.

Tanja Rohini Bisgaard, December 2017

Still Waters

Kimberly Christensen

The aftershocks of the slammed door reverberated in Petra's ears as her lover thumped down the stairs, past the little teahouse on the ground floor, and out of the building. Petra finished drying the last of the dishes, then wiped down the old butcher-block countertop, scrubbing at the same worn stains as if another pass of the sponge would finally remove them from the wood. The silence was broken only by the rasping of sponge against butcher block. A small gladness flickered to life in the silence and pushed away the tightness that ringed her rib cage. Petra almost started to hum.

Working her way through the living room, she adjusted the stack of books on the coffee table, lining up their spines then plumbing the whole pile so the long edges paralleled the edge of the table. She tidied Bethari's jumble of shoes, matching each to its mate as she set them in a careful line along the floorboards next to her own. She fought the compulsion to kick them into disarray and send them flying down the stairs after their owner.

Petra's sharp tongue had chased the woman off this morning, impatience finally bubbling over at Bethari's suggestion that picked green beans were an insufficient breakfast. Bethari had grabbed her raincoat and slammed the front door with a meaningful glance over her shoulder. A look that said they were too old for such arguments, and Petra's temper needed to lose its edges. As if Petra were some damned bottle of wine that should mellow with age.

She didn't even think mellowing with age was possible in 2047.

Before the whales had died, she and Janie might have philosophized about the possibilities of mellowing with age while living within a dystopia, laughing to themselves about the ironic nature of such a conversation when held from the comfort of a cat-covered couch. Before the whales died, they might have determined there were four ways of coping with the real-life dystopia of the modern world: addiction, suicide, anarchy, and hiding under the bed. They might have debated whether addiction was the same as suicide, just slower.

They never considered the slowest death: the one that comes when one loses her will to live.

Technically, Janie had died in the Pandemic of 2041, but Petra counted her death as having lasted four years, long enough to make it an epoch in the geology of her own lifespan. For four years, she had watched Janie withdraw into the private nautilus of her innermost self, curling her thoughts and dreams and essence into that smooth spiral of a shell. When Janie crossed over into the afterlife, Petra briefly wondered if she would miss her wife, as she'd grown used to the company of her own thoughts. Instead, grief pushed her down a long tunnel of darkness.

Petra flirted with the darkness—contemplated what it might feel like to exhale the tendrils of her own essence into the waiting void. But she never had really understood suicide, whether by action or addiction or slow wasting, so she just kept getting out of bed and doing the necessary things. In this way, she settled into widowhood and the gentle individuality of living alone. She had been one cat away from a perfect, self-contained life.

Then, with an easy laugh and the gentle caress of her graceful brown hand, Bethari had completely disrupted that. Her warm palms easily withstood the sharpest of Petra's prickles, and she had the sense, on days like today, to give Petra space to sort things out. Except, even with six years of widowhood behind her, Petra was no closer to mellowing into a fine wine. She wondered if vinegar was a more realistic goal.

Petra smoothed the coverlet in her room, squaring its corners and adjusting the pillows. She plucked several of Bethari's stockings off the floor and tossed them into the laundry pile. Next, she swiped at the bookcase with her shirtsleeve, checking for traces of dust and finding none. She sighed—loudly—pushing at the surrounding silence with her breath. More silence responded.

She finally grabbed her favorite gray raincoat, with its soft fleece lining. She slipped on a pair of comfortable walking shoes—the kind Janie used to say resembled baked potatoes—and emerged into the dark, drizzly morning. Hood up, head down, she headed west to her thinking place. She let the door slam loudly behind her.

The bleached white bones rose starkly against the gray of the February sky, the giant rib cages resting on the sand like an armada of shipwrecks worn down to their frames by the constant assault of the elements. Petra trailed her hand along the rain-beaded bones, following the weaving path that carried her from skeleton to skeleton along this pebbly stretch of Puget Sound beach. This was the Boneyard of the Giants, the final resting place of eighteen orca skeletons. The last of the Southern Resident orcas had washed ashore here in February, 2037, dying in plain sight of a horrified Seattle, whose people were still coming to grips with the ongoing disaster called climate change.

This marked the beginning of the four-year dying epoch, according to Petra's timeline.

If she stared at the skeletons and let her vision go fuzzy, she could still see the whales as they had looked when they started beaching themselves on this stretch of rocky sand. The shadows of the whales disappeared as Petra blinked hard, which brought their skeletons back into sharp focus. She took a deep breath of damp salt air before continuing down the path to her favorite bench near the skeleton of J-47, Notch. After a halfhearted wipe at the pooled rain on the bench, she sat down.

"Damn it all," she muttered. "I don't want to deal with this."

And she didn't. Not her argument with Bethari, or its converse, growing old alone. Not dead whales on a stretch of beach. Not everything and everyone who had died since.

The J-Pod orcas had felt like Petra and Janie's whales from the moment they'd first spotted them off the side of one of Puget Sound's ubiquitous ferryboats, but true Northwesterners told them that ferryboat sightings didn't count. It was a couple of years before they understood why.

On this portentous day, they had pushed their kayak through the small waves that lapped the shore and paddled out into the quiet of the summer morning. A few cormorants called, circling overhead, scouting for breakfast. Janie and Petra paddled in rhythm, the sound of their paddles steady as a heartbeat. As they drew near Alki Point, they stopped paddling and enjoyed a few moments of rest. Small waves licked their kayak.

Janie pointed at a stand of madrona trees that lined the coast before handing Petra a pair of binoculars.

"Eagle," she said quietly, gesturing to the upper branches of a particularly large tree.

Petra followed the trajectory of her finger until she saw the flash of the bald eagle's white head. She had just begun to focus the binoculars when a blast of air pierced the stillness and bathed them in a mist of fish-scented, orca-warm exhalation.

"Holy shit," they breathed, as the triangle of a dorsal fin skimmed through the water so close they could have touched it, unevenly black where scars and pocks marked it. A notch had been chipped out along its leading edge. The two sat in silence as the dorsal fin was joined by two more, the three orcas tumbling back and forth through the water, just out of reach of the kayak, which swayed with the animals' movements.

The notch-finned whale changed course, swimming in a large circle around the kayak, angled on its side so its large unblinking eye stared up at them through the clear water. Another orca dove beneath them, then surfaced with a puff of air so close that it bejeweled their hair with briny dewdrops and flecks of lung mucus. Petra's heart raced as she measured the vastness of the whales against the twelve feet of kayak. She had never felt so much like prey.

Her knuckles ached where she was strangling her oar. She loosened them, breathing slowly and evenly to clear her head as the whales darted back and forth a few feet beneath the surface. They twisted in the water, letting it roll across their sleek bodies as they propelled themselves with efficient thrusts of their tails. Once the throbbing of her own heartbeat receded, she could even make out the faint sonar clicks the orcas sent racing ahead of them.

Just as her heartbeat evened, the whales raced at the kayak, twisting out of its path inches before impact. She and Janie braced themselves against the heaving wake that threatened to overturn them. The notched whale doubled back, swimming once around them in a great arc, the large eye peering at them from just below the surface, and the toothy mouth open in a mockery of a smile.

"It's messing with us," Petra whispered to Janie.

"Maybe it's showing off for its friends," Janie whispered back.

"I just want it to know I'm not a seal."

"Me too."

Notch continued the game for a few more minutes: circling, diving, surfacing, but never once bumping the boat. Then it charged at the kayak one last time before turning sharply and torpedoing toward the open water. The other two whales sped along behind it, the smallest breaching with a mighty flop, sending a slap of water rollicking toward the kayak one last time. The two women grabbed the sides of the kayak as it bounced in the whale's wake and kept holding on long after the last ripple had passed.

"Oh, my God," Janie said. "That was fucking amazing."

"I thought it was going to tip us over for sure."

"I didn't. I think it just wanted to know what we're made of. To see if we're orca worthy."

Janie slapped the water with the flat of her paddle, showering them both with cold droplets, through which they ululated full throated, bouncing the sounds off each ripple in the water and every sharp-edged leaf that hung from the trees along the coast. Their shouts returned to Petra's ears like sonar clicks, and for a moment, she knew the location of every fish, bird, and dandelion.

They hadn't stayed long on the water after that, paddling furiously toward a remote part of the coastline. The kayak scraped against the gravel beach, its back end still bobbing in the water as they leapt out of it, after which they tumbled onto a hastily spread picnic blanket where they made loud, frantic love. Petra's orgasm cut deep—sharp as leaf edges, bird feathers, whale teeth, splaying open her vital organs for the ravens to feast upon. She didn't even try to fight them.

Long minutes later, her wits slowly coalesced around the steady pounding of Janie's heartbeat.

They both glowed for weeks.

Petra tried hard to hold onto her memory of that day, but the wind off the sound chilled her back into February, where she sat next to the skeleton of that same whale that may or may not have found them orca worthy. She rubbed at the tears that bit her cheeks. February was her hardest month, the dark days beckoning her to follow them down the grief tunnel again and the cold layering itself around the familiar ache of loss.

"I miss you, Janie," she said to the whale bones.

The bones answered with silence.

On February 6, 2037, the early-morning tide deposited the first three orcas onto the pebbled beach at Carkeek Park. It was the wrong time of year for orcas to be this far south, and news of the stranding spread quickly through the city. Petra and Janie heard it as they lay in bed, listening to public radio. There was no decision that needed to be made. They simply rose, pulled on layers of clothing, emptied the cabinet of energy bars, and went to see what they could do to help.

The wind blew bitterly across the Puget Sound, freezing the surface of the tide pools and coating the edges of stones, nostrils, and blowholes in icy rime. It also blew in more whales. The veterinary team immediately put Petra and Janie to work, handing them buckets and sponges, with instructions to keep the whales wet while they worked out a plan for tube-feeding them or hauling them back into the water—anything but leaving them here to die. The women rubbed the whales tenderly, whispering words of encouragement to them, and trying to ignore the worrisome ease with which they discerned each individual rib. They joined the prayers of the Coast Salish people, who arrived to care for the whales' physical and spiritual needs. They experimented with sheathing the whales in foil blankets, layered over damp towels, to protect them against the drying, bitter wind.

A mass stranding of orcas in the dead of winter was uncharted territory.

On their second day of volunteering, as they crossed the slick metal bridge that connected the parking lot with the beach, Janie's knees bowed beneath her. She cried out, pointing to the string of new whales that had washed up in the early-morning hours.

"No, no, no!" she cried. "Not Notch!"

Janie recovered her footing and sprinted down the stairs to his side, Petra trailing behind her. By the time she caught up, Janie already had displaced the volunteer who had been tending to Notch–Whale J-47, Male, 27 years old. She was crooning softly to him as she sponged his side. He stared at her with one unblinking eye.

"Oh, buddy," Petra said, resting a hand on his side.

"Pet, we have to save him. We have to get him back into the water." Janie thrust a bucket into her hands. "Start sponging. I'm going to talk with the lead vet."

Spots reddened the centers of Janie's cheeks when she returned and wordlessly grabbed a sponge from the bucket. She moved to Notch's other side, and soon Petra caught snippets of melodies rising across his tall back as Janie sang to him—the same songs she had once sung to Petra as they had lain in bed in the throes of new love. Here in the open air, Janie's voice cut through the cold and settled like a blanket of loss over Petra, who already knew in her bones how this would end. The twenty-three souls washed up on this beach were not going to return to the sea.

Janie cheered each time Notch released breath from his blowhole. Petra felt the trembling in his sides, worried over the increasing time between each breath, observed the dulling of his pupils. She heard the crying of veterinarians and volunteers when they announced the death of the first whale—the littlest one, called Bear. If Janie understood the cries, she gave no sign. She leaned her head against Notch's flank and continued to sing, her voice now raw and raspy.

On the third day, Petra took more breaks. She walked among the dying—she was learning to recognize the telltale dulling of their open eyes and a peculiar, almost imperceptible sagging that shaped their bellies where they flattened against the sand.

"When my time has come," she prayed over them, "and impermanence and death have caught up with me... When the breath ceases and the body and mind go their separate ways..."

She blessed them as she walked. Blessed the gifts their lives had brought. Blessed the ways in which their deaths might benefit other living beings. The crows and the crabs waited at the edges, ready for such beneficence.

Petra's hands ached, the constant wet and cold chapping them to the point of bleeding. Fissures cracked her heart as well, worn raw by bearing witness to so much death. She knew she had to stay until the last of the whales had died. It was only right that the humans who had caused this extinction stay to witness its horrible finality. But she deeply, deeply wished to go home, with Janie, and find comfort in her arms—away from all this.

Notch died at dusk on that third day. His last breath was a prolonged sigh that bore Janie's wailing above it, her grief rising and falling until it had wrapped itself around the body of every whale and pierced the benumbed heart of each person gathered on that sad beach. Soft crying surrounded Petra, her own tears stinging as they rolled down her wind-raw cheeks. Janie keened and keened as she knelt beside Notch, her hands pressed against his side, her face tipped toward the descending darkness. Slowly the rescue crews returned to motion, comforting the last few whales, all of which would soon join Notch in death.

Petra knew Janie wouldn't leave Notch's side that night, so she tucked her into a sleeping bag and sat beside her. Eventually Janie cried herself to sleep, her back to Petra and her palm pressed against Notch's cold, rubbery skin. She was in the same position when Petra returned the next morning, after having gone home to feed the cats and crying herself into exhaustion under a hot shower.

On day four, the final whale—J-17, Princess Angeline—died, and when the cold wind blew this time, it settled in the marrow of Petra's bones. She pulled her jacket up higher, zipping its collar over her mouth and nose. She rubbed her hands together as she stood next to Janie, who sat huddled in her sleeping bag next to Notch, staring out at the horizon with red-rimmed eyes.

"Janie, love," she said. "We can't help him anymore. We should go home."

"There's no reason to go."

"What do you want to do?" asked Petra. "Stay here?"

Janie shrugged.

"They're dead, Janie," Petra said softly. "There's nothing more we can do."

"We can keep the birds away."

Petra glanced down the shoreline. Crows lingered in every tree, darting in to rip off hunks of whale flesh, which they carried back to the high branches.

"The birds are just doing what birds do."

"Carrion beasts," Janie spat.

When Petra reached for her arm, Janie turned away.

"Am I just supposed to go home? Go back to work?" Janie demanded. "Pretend this didn't happen? That we didn't just witness an extinction?"

Petra had no good answer.

"What do you want to do?" she asked.

Janie shook her head. "I don't know."

She turned back to Notch and picked up a stick so she could fend off scavengers. She stood up and circled the whale's body, her body tensed with purpose as she scanned the ground for crabs and the sky for crows. She traded her stick for a longer one, one that let her swing at a crow that tried to settle on Notch's back.

"Have some respect!" she shouted at a girl who was taking a selfie with one of the whales and chased her off with her stick raised. The girl fled across the bridge, and Janie gave a chortle of victory before resuming her circling.

When the researchers started performing full necropsies on the whales, it proved too much for most of the volunteers. By twos and threes they left, plugging their ears against the sound of the chainsaws—their wind-burned, tear-reddened faces turned miserably away from the cold. Most didn't look back as they crossed the bridge over the train tracks to return to their cars. Petra shuffled across the bridge with them. In the parking lot, she rummaged in the trunk for hot packs, which she snapped and pressed into Janie's freezing hands on the beach. She made the trip to the car three more times before she finally convinced Janie to come home—which she would only do after the veterinarians had necropsied Notch. She held his tailfin the entire time.

Petra never would forget the sound of chainsaw on bone.

The next morning, Petra and Janie awoke early. They huddled beneath their duvet in the semidarkness, watching the sky grow lighter behind the barren maple outside their window. A flock of chickadees alighted on the branches, in search of forgotten seeds. Petra rose and lumbered to the kitchen to make coffee. She brought a steaming mug back to the bedroom for Janie, only to find her dressed from head to toe in black and searching for her keys.

"Where are you going?" Petra asked.

Janie took the coffee from Petra and poured it into a travel mug without comment. Petra followed her to the Subaru.

"Janie?

"I won't leave them there to rot, alone except for the crabs and crows."

"What are you going to do?"

"Protect them. Mourn. Not move on as if everything is normal."

Her words were a challenge, Petra knew.

"It's not normal," she agreed. "I'll come after I get some work done."

"Bring your walking stick," Janie instructed Petra. "You can help keep the birds away."

They fell into a rhythm, Janie departing in the early hours to keep watch over Notch alongside the Coast Salish protectors who had set up camp on the beach. Petra put in the bare minimum of time necessary to keep her teahouse running before joining Janie at the beach. She felt badly for leaning so heavily on her employees and guiltily made phone calls from the shelter of the restroom to help keep things running. At least working on the business kept her from fretting about

21

Janie's mental state. She hoped that time would bring closure.

Several days into this routine, a team of wildlife management workers arrived with tugboats and wetsuited crews to drag the whale carcasses out to sea for disposal. They arrived early and without announcement, quickly looping cables around two of the whales. Janie already was keeping vigil over Notch, her stick in hand. Petra had been following a path across the beach that had emerged over the past week, winding from whale to whale.

"No!" Janie shouted. "You can't take them! You can't!"

She ran at them, waving her walking stick like a bludgeon. Petra raced after her, catching her as she reached the group. They stepped back from Janie, hands outstretched, and looked to Petra to save them from the madwoman.

"She thinks their skeletons should remain here as a memorial," Petra said.

"Nice idea," one of the crew said. "But the decision's already been made."

"You don't understand," said another. "The decomposition process is unsanitary. It could close the park for half a year at least. Best to let us haul them away."

He signaled to the people on the tugboats, who increased their throttles. The motors strained as the boats pulled at the whales. The wetsuited workers pushed the bodies as the boats pulled. Slowly the whales scraped along beach, leaving chunks of flesh among the rocks and mussels. Janie kept screaming for them to stop, but they didn't listen. When Petra took her by the arm and tried to lead her away, she dug her heels into the sand. Tears streamed down her face. She watched until she no longer could see the bodies bobbing along behind the boats.

The Coast Salish protectors formed a human chain along the edge of the beach to prevent anyone from attempting to haul off the remaining twenty-one whales. Janie canvassed the beach, talking to the clusters of visitors who had come to see the dead whales, encouraging them to film everything. Wildlife management gave up for the day.

Three more carcasses were hauled off in the cover of night after police arrested anyone who wouldn't leave and cleared their encampment.

The following day, the tribes filed an injunction, which—with tremendous public support—halted the removal of the bodies, at least for the time being. But none of the activists trusted the government to leave the bodies alone. The Coast Salish set up camp once again, and Janie joined them, sleeping in a tent on the beach.

As the wildlife experts had predicted, the whales truly became a disgusting sight, and the stench became nearly untenable, even for the activists who persevered despite it. Although they covered their faces with bandanas and breathed through their mouths, the vomit smell of decay clung to them and choked them. Scavenging birds had devoured the flesh along the spines, exposing the knobby vertebrae. The rest of the flesh, now that it wasn't connected at the top, was sliding toward the sand in gelatinous strings as warm spells hastened the decomposition rate.

At this point, only a few people walked among the carcasses. Janie declared that she would remain there until the Seattle City Council declared it an official memorial. She woke before dawn each morning to crunch along the path—

carrying signs, singing protest songs, or calling the council with her demands. The tech company she worked for offered Janie a mental health leave, but she was unwilling to sign the forms Petra printed and hauled down to the beach. She lost her job.

Petra juggled managing the teahouse, caring for the cats, and bringing dinner to Janie every night. She watched as the softness melted from Janie's curves. She worried over the ease with which she could count her ribs, dreamed of Janie's flesh falling from her bones and puddling around her feet. Sometimes she lay down beside her in the little tent, working to fall asleep despite the miasma of gases coming off the rotting whales. She usually awoke alone, Janie already at Notch's side. Eventually the city council approved the memorial, and the other Grief Walkers—as they had come to call themselves—trickled home to their former anonymous lives. Janie didn't come home for three days.

The stench of the carcasses still clung to Janie's hair. She tucked a greasy lock behind her ear and looked out through the open bedroom window. She shook her head slowly, never looking directly at Petra.

"What do you want from me, Petra?" she asked.

Her voice was worryingly flat. She refused counseling. She refused to look for a new job. She spent hours staring at nothing. Even the cats had given up on getting a response from her, though every now and then one climbed on her bony lap and kneaded her legs until he drew blood.

"I want you to get better," Petra said.

"From extinction? I don't know how to get better from extinction."

"Me either, but we have to try."

Janie didn't respond.

"Damn it, Janie," Petra yelled. "Get mad again! Find something to fight for!"

Janie's eyes tracked a junco on the tree outside, but she said nothing. Petra ran a hand through her hair then sat next to Janie on the bed. She took Janie's hand in hers, staring at her until at last Janie looked back. Janie smiled a small, sad smile.

"Janie, what can we do? What would help? We could help other orcas. The whole species hasn't gone extinct. We could sell everything and move north. Join a research team or something."

The sad smile grew sadder then faded. Janie shook her head.

"No. I won't go and witness more death. These were enough."

It was like watching someone drown in slow motion, the still waters of grief just closing over her wife's submerging head. There was no flailing involved. No calls for rescue. Janie simply sank right before her eyes.

Months crawled by this way. Their friends spoke of Janie in hushed tones, as if she had cancer or some other unmentionable disease. They stopped coming over. Petra started going out on her own—she just couldn't take the silence.

The months dragged into years. They lost friends. Petra made new ones without Janie and didn't bring them home. But most nights she worked late, climbing up the stairs from the teahouse to an already-sleeping household. Four years she lived like that, watching her wife die of a broken heart.

They both got sick. Petra knew, as soon as the diagnosis was confirmed, how it would end. The pandemic flu didn't spare the very old or the very young, and while there were no official statistics on survival rates for the brokenhearted, Petra's prediction proved true. Janie died without a fight. Her lungs filled with fluid and she died. Days later, Petra was released from the hospital with a bag of antibiotics and a box of ashes. It was a sudden, cruel end to something years in the making.

After Petra had spread Janie's ashes near the whale bones, she briefly considered running away, but she couldn't very well move to Alaska and join a research team without Janie. That had never been a real plan anyway, only a desperate idea concocted to try to lure Janie back to the land of the living. No, that wasn't a real plan. So Petra just kept doing what she'd been doing: running the teahouse, watching junk television, spending time with friends. She did all this as if Janie were still waiting for her in their apartment.

The bones were stripped clean now, ten years later, bleached white monuments to a fallen species. Petra stood up and walked over to Notch's side, resting her hand on his bones in the place where she remembered Janie resting hers. She could almost feel Janie's warm hand beneath hers, nearly close enough for her to grasp and to lead home to the tidy, quiet apartment she had kept for the past six years.

"Choose life, Janie," she whispered. "Choose me."

Petra stood there until the light changed and the wind picked up. She trudged back over the bridge that spanned the railroad tracks and led her to the park entrance. The walk home was mostly downhill, thank the goddess. She was so weary. She just wanted to climb into bed and sleep for a week. She didn't want to talk to people, let alone a lover.

By the time she made it home, darkness had fallen. The sign in the front window of the teahouse had been flipped to CLOSED, but candles still glowed brightly through the windowpanes, illuminating the condensation that framed the edges of the glass. Petra saw Bethari's silhouette just inside the front door, her head bent over a book. Waiting for her.

She contemplated going around the back and sneaking into the apartment up the rear staircase. But she'd been trying to go back for six years. Or at least to not go forward.

Hell, she hadn't even gotten a cat.

Petra took a deep breath and promised herself she would get a cat tomorrow.

And then she pushed open the front door.

A Modern Cronkite

Richard Friedman

Mother called the meeting to order. A group of her supporters waited to hear her speak. As she began, a crowd filled the corridor that ran from the forest to the Cuyahoga River. "Thank you to our hosts and all of you who traveled long distances to be here. It's a solemn day, and despite our anger, frustration, and mixed feelings about the current situation, I've made a decision and want you to hear it straight from me, not through a series of underground messages or back channels spread through the woods. We're going to war with the enemy, and nothing short of victory is acceptable. The actions required to win go beyond any scale witnessed by human beings. Millions of you will die on the battlefield; in backyards; in cities, in forests; in streams, lakes, and rivers—wherever the fight leads us. There can be no peace or truce. The enemy's prayers will go unanswered. We will fight until we achieve total destruction. We'll take back our land or risk perishing forever. Now go   spread the word to the rest of us. Plan A is in effect and begins immediately."

I wasn't special. I went to Syracuse University and majored in journalism. Thousands of recent graduates were scattered around the country, hoping to land a job writing for a newspaper. I wanted to see my byline in print. The business model of that industry changed long ago, and I joined the crowd searching for "clicks." The more clicks, the more cash, the higher the salary. Ugh, that wasn't why I studied journalism. I wanted to be the modern version of Walter Cronkite, the esteemed journalist from my grandparents' era. Most of my friends didn't know who he was and wouldn't recognize his face in a photograph.

I eventually took a job at *Lake County News Herald*, a small newspaper in Northeast Ohio, a bit east of Cleveland, and the birthplace of former President Garfield. As Cronkite used to say in his sign-off from his television news show, "And that's the way it is." This is my account of the most bizarre—and likely last—few months of my life. I will continue to provide updates until my strength runs out. I pray this document proves useful to whoever finds it. And that's the way it was for me, Spencer Parker.

I was the reporter sent to cover local oil and gas spills, wind farms, hydroelectric generators, pipeline leaks, and a heart-wrenching story about a bunch of Boy Scouts who used their bicycles to power a battery pack for a kid with cancer whose parents didn't have the money to pay the electric bill. That was a tough assignment. As my reputation gained traction, I became the go-to guy for environmental news in this part of Ohio. I buried myself in books, signed up for graduate-level classes at Case Western Reserve University in Cleveland, and knew more details of the hazards of air, water, and land pollution than anyone I knew.

It was early 2047, and President Burke successfully followed the Republican agenda that continued to send the country backward in every meaningful environmental way.

Burke stripped power away from the Environmental Protection Agency and allowed Congress to increase fracking and offshore drilling. When President Trump withdrew the United States from the Paris Climate Agreement in 2017, the consequences rippled throughout the world, casting the United States as a global pariah in the fight against climate change and global Warming. Without American ingenuity and effort, China and India lost their will to meet air-quality deadlines, and citizens in Europe and Asia continued to have days when leaving the house without wearing an air-purifying mask brought the risk of respiratory ailments.

Not even a massive oil spill in the Gulf of Mexico, one nearly as bad as British Petroleum's Deepwater Horizon disaster in 2010, swayed President Burke from abandoning oil and coal as the best means to energize the economy and keep gas prices low. He filled his cabinet with like-minded thinkers while environmentalists continued to rally support to stand firmly against the assaults on every facet of the environment. The battle proved fruitless. Oil ran through newly built pipelines across the country, bringing new jobs, along with the risk of catastrophic environmental disasters. It wasn't a question of "if" a pipeline would leak; it was a question of "when" and how much damage it would cause. They did leak, causing the Mississippi disaster of 2036, killing 345 people and costing a billion dollars to clean up. The rich petroleum executives paid no consideration to the inevitable forthcoming disasters and raked in big bonuses for their efforts. The country hadn't been this divided since the Civil War. Extremists on both ends of environment battled in court, in Congress, and occasionally in back alleys. Gun violence soared to record highs, and Democrats couldn't find a strong leader to compete in the upcoming election, dooming their prospects to reclaim the White House.

It was at this moment when I received the call that changed my life.

I had just finished binge-watching another Netflix nature series when my cell phone rang. If a new caller came in—and that happened frequently—the song "Who Are You?" played on my phone, and a 3-D image of the ancient rock 'n' roll group The Who popped up in my living room. The vision was so real I could practically bang on Keith Moon's drum kit.

"Hello," I said. Did I mention I considered myself a brilliant conversationalist? I still needed work on my opening line. Perhaps that's why I was sitting there by myself on a Friday night.

A woman's voice responded, "Is this Mr. Parker?"

For a moment, I thought this was my lucky night. I mean, how many single guys receive calls from women late at night if it's not for sex? Unfortunately, this call wasn't one of them.

"Yes, this is he. Who's calling, please?" You can tell by my smooth style that I was reeling her in now. And polite too. Girls love when guys say "please" and "thank you." I'd better start chilling the white wine.

There was a long pause, and then the woman said, "I'd rather not say over the phone. Can we meet somewhere tomorrow?"

The reporter in me knew the answer was yes. It was always yes. Her voice was extraordinary. I couldn't tell if it was her tone, timbre, delivery, or the overall sense of calmness she projected, but I knew I had to meet her.

"Where should we meet?" I asked.

"At the concession stand at Blossom Music Center. Three o'clock sharp. Come by yourself or you won't find me."

I said, "Okay," and the call abruptly ended. I returned the wine to the rack. I looked at the thermometer outside the window, and it read twenty-three degrees Fahrenheit. Not awful for early January; in fact, the average temperature in January is one degree warmer compared to thirty years ago, but it still wasn't the type of weather to venture to an outdoor amphitheater. Blossom was widely known for music concerts, the summer venue for the Cleveland Orchestra, and the location of my high school graduation.

The next afternoon, I bundled up and made the hour-long journey from my home in Cleveland Heights to Cuyahoga Falls, the site of my secret meeting…with someone, about something. The intrigue was killing me. I parked my hydrogen-powered car and walked the half mile to the concession stand.

I checked my watch—yes, I still wore one. I arrived five minutes early. That was a habit of mine. Come early, be prepared, and get a jump on the competition.

The place was vacant, except for me, and hopefully my mystery date.

Little did I know how the world would change in the next four months.

"Hello!" I said. The word didn't carry far in the expanse. A short distance from my location was the huge grassy lawn that held fifteen thousand concertgoers and led to a covered amphitheater that seated several thousand more spectators.

I repeated my greeting, this time with more gusto, cupping my hands to the corners of my mouth in an effort to extend the sound. "Hel-loooo!" I called out, dragging out the end of the word, hoping someone would hear me. If a security guard was minding the grounds, he wasn't nearby.

"Back here."

"Huh? Where are you?"

The voice said, "You're the star reporter and you can't figure that out? Maybe I chose the wrong man for this job."

"A sarcastic spirit, just the story I dreamed of. Maybe I'll call the squad from *Ghostbusters* to assist me."

"Come back into the woods," she said. "I prepared a spot for you."

Undaunted, I passed the concession stand and found a metal folding chair in the middle of a cleared-out section of the woods. Tall pine trees circled the open area. As I sat in the chair, I felt like a criminal waiting for the FBI to blast a light in my face and ask me where I was on September 21st.

"Thank you for coming, Mr. Parker. I hope you're up to the task."

Her voice was firm yet calming. "Secrecy evidently is important to you," I said. "But I want to see who I'm speaking with."

"At this point, that's not possible."

I asked, "What should I call you?"

A male voice from another section of the woods said, "Why don't you call her Mother?" I could have sworn I heard laughter, but it faded quickly.

She said, "Fine, call me Mother."

How are they able to hide so well in the middle of the day? I wondered, then said, "So, Mother, why the clandestine meeting? Why drag me out here in the middle of winter? Couldn't we have met at Geraci's for a pepperoni pizza?"

With that question, uproar arose from the woods. Although I couldn't decipher the words, there was no mistaking my question had drawn their anger.

"Is this a meeting for vegetarians or something?" I asked.

Mother said, "Let's proceed, shall we?"

My eyes scanned the area, looking for shadows or movement. I found nothing.

"Mr. Parker," she continued, "you have a long track record of trying to protect the environment, and on behalf of the assembled group here today, I'd like to thank you. There are millions on our side. Unfortunately, we're outnumbered by apathy at the highest levels of government. The attempts to solve our environmental crisis over many decades have failed catastrophically. All that effort has led to more anguish and turmoil. Nothing changes without drastic action. For all of us gathered here today, all I see is despair and heartache."

I couldn't see anyone, and clearly that was by design. I felt their presence, though—watching me, listening to me. I assumed they'd brought me here for a reason. I couldn't imagine how this woman had built a sizable force without the intelligence community getting wind of it, unless they were part of it too. The pieces of the story didn't fit the puzzle. So as any good reporter would, I asked questions. I fired them off rapidly, foolishly not giving Mother a chance to reply.

"What do you want from me? Why didn't you call CNN or Fox News? Where are you from? Haven't you heard China is moving away from fossil fuels at a record pace? Coal-burning fossil fuel plants are on the way out!"

Right now I can hear the words of my sophomore-year journalism teacher, Professor Tunnicliffe, in the back of my head: *That's a bad job out of you, Mr. Parker.*

Mother replied, "There are millions of us. We're not all standing here, with our feet planted on the ground, but we're ready to fight. The planet is heating up, and I've reached my breaking point. I could sit back, watch the seas rise higher, and let nature take its course. That would take a millennium, and there's no guarantee I would achieve my goal. Global warming is a small part of my concern. Is anyone stopping the flow of pesticides into creeks and rivers? Tell me, Mr. Parker, why does the ocean continue to fill with plastic at unprecedented rates? Why do people need to check the Air Alert Channel to see if they can drive their cars to work or need to wear masks to walk the downtown streets of a city? I could continue all day. You appreciate my concerns more than most. I feel like I'm preaching to the choir."

"I don't have all the answers," I told her. "Fixing our environmental problems goes way beyond my humble knowledge. I feel helpless. How can the actions of one individual change the world? I've tried to make an impact locally. I started a program to help clean up the Cuyahoga River. I hope others will do the same in their communities, and perhaps, bit by bit, we'll beat the pollution problem once and for all."

Guffaws and snorts of disbelief echoed from the woods.

"Your efforts are noteworthy," Mother continued, "and that's precisely why I chose you for this task, which I'll explain in short order. Unfortunately, we don't have time to delay taking action. I owe it to my constituency. This simply can't wait. It breaks my heart...it really does. There's no other logical choice. In the simplest of terms, this is war, Mr. Parker. It's us against them, and my side will prevail, no matter how many lives it costs."

"You're saying the ends justify the means."

"That is correct," she replied.

"How many soldiers do you have at your disposal?"

She said, "Enough to do the job."

"What kind of weapons do you plan on using?"

"The kind that can't be stopped."

"That's an ominous phrase," I told her. "Do you have nukes or chemical weapons?"

Mother replied, "Nukes and chemicals would destroy everything. That's the furthest thing from my mind. I'm not explaining my tactics to you. You'll see for yourself."

"I see this line of questioning is getting me nowhere, so I'll get to the point. Why am I here?"

"You're a journalist. You have the means to let the world know what's happening."

"I can't waltz into the office and tell the boss there's a lady in charge of an army living in the woods near Blossom Music Center, allegedly coming to attack us. I don't know when or why, who, or how they plan to do it. That's an outrageous story. Nobody would print that without a second source to confirm it."

"What do you need to confirm it?" she asked. "A bunch of dead bodies?"

Kiddingly, I said, "That would be a good start. It would be better if you came to the office and sat down with the editor in chief and the owner of the paper. I don't even know what you look like. Can you sit next to me? At least do that for me, and I'll have something to come to them with. For all I know, this is a prank by one of my old fraternity brothers. Did Neal or Joe put you up to this?"

More wrestling noises came from the woods. A baritone voice said, "I told you this was a waste of time. He won't do it. You said he'd print the story and warn the public about what was going to happen. But he's a chicken, like that little guy sitting next to you."

The accused answered, "I'm not afraid. Not everyone is as tough as you are. I'm willing to put my neck on the line too. I'll do whatever I can to help."

Mother said, "Come now, boys. Don't get your feathers ruffled. Let's be mature in front of our guest. War is no laughing matter, and this is the last one I'm going to witness. Mr. Parker, you can go, write whatever you wish. I'm sure we'll meet again. The next time, though, it'll be you who reaches out to me."

"I'll see what I can do," I told her. "You realize this sounds crazy, right? You and a few of your friends are bringing a war against America."

Mother said, "Mr. Parker, it's not only America! This is a global battle for supremacy of the planet. I have contacts on every continent, ready to make their move."

I rubbed my hands together to warm them. "Right. Sure, lady, the entire world. That won't make my job any easier. I suppose you have a plan to eliminate the one billion people living in China? Have you been to India lately? It's pretty crowded there." I paused, "Well, listen, this has been fascinating. I'm outta here."

I got back into my car and headed north on Route 8, trying to figure out a plausible way to verbalize this experience. I clicked on satellite radio and listened to the BBC; a reporter was describing the ongoing driving ban in London due to excessive smog. The PMI ratings had soared to over 375, and doctors in the United Kingdom urged citizens with respiratory problems to stay indoors. The whole time, I couldn't shake this woman's fervent desire for retribution. She was either a great actress like Meryl Streep, or certifiable. I needed to speak to her again to determine her truthfulness. I decided to let a little time pass and see if anything unfolded in the news.

While I drove, the meeting in the woods continued— something I learned about much later.

Mother presented solemn news to the big guys standing in the back of the woods. "I want you to hear this directly from my mouth. You will die in this confrontation. And you won't fire a single shot. You will perish in large numbers. It will be on a scale of unparalleled magnitude. Do not despair. Your offspring will repopulate the planet. They'll be proud, appreciating the sacrifice you made on their behalf."

They looked on with confusion until one spoke up. "It's easy for you to tell us not to despair! Are you sure this is the best way? I thought we'd fight the enemy with fire and burn them to the ground. Or at worst, die with bravery until the bitter end. I don't understand. What's your plan? We won't win if we curl up and die like old grapes on the vine. I thought I might live to tell of my legendary battle. I'm only in my early thirties!"

Mother was stern. "I have a plan, and it will work. You must trust me. I know your families well. I saw what the enemy did to them. Cut down in the prime of their lives. Others will tell the tales of your glorious victory. Not one family among you will escape death. Young or old, weak or strong, black or white. Everyone will share the pain. This is not the moment to doubt me. I'm your leader, and I know what is best in the long run. Your selfless acts of suicide will lead the charge to victory."

"Suicide?" many of them yelled in unison. This was not the plan they envisioned.

Mother asked, "Do any among you wish to challenge my blueprint?"

After a brief delay, someone spoke. "Mother, we realize you are wise. Suicide seems out of character for us. And how will it help us win? You haven't explained the plan at all. You want us to lay down our lives without telling us why—that's the ultimate leap of faith. Some of us can trace our roots back to the cradle of civilization. For us, well, it's difficult to imagine going out that way. We don't see how suici—"

Mother interrupted with a measured tone. "The goal is victory. I'm not interested in style points. You can't comprehend the entirety of my strategy. I can't go from town to town explaining it to everyone. I've thought this through and anticipated every possible scenario, and this is the best way. Have I let you down yet?"

She didn't wait for an answer.

"I would never let you down. I might be guilty of waiting too patiently to seize this opportunity. But that's all in the past. We have heroes at our disposal—heroes who will win the battle for control of the land and the sea. One by one, with no recourse to stop our assault, the enemy will perish. At first, they won't show concern. As the casualties escalate, a few will reach out to make a peaceful settlement. It's too late for that. I don't want you to forget what's happened to you. They say time heals all wounds. Time doesn't heal their grievous attacks on our way of life. They stole your land! Why? Greed! There was plenty to share if they showed a modicum of care or concern. They wrote laws to protect us and made false promises. Now those lies are coming home to roost. We're on the threshold of reclaiming our world. Military leaders will be powerless to stop us. As they grow desperate, their resolve to fight will diminish. They'll turn against each other as society falls into anarchy. When food and water shortages reach their peak, governments will declare martial law and entrust their armies to control the population. Their demise will be swift, and I'll claim supremacy over all living inhabitants and ensure our rightful place at the top."

Not everyone was impressed with her bluster. They spoke softly, hoping to avoid her sharp hearing. "I think the power is going to her head, don't you?"

Another said, "Talk about an ego. How did we let it come to this?"

Mother said, "I hear the conversation in the back. This isn't about my ego. This battle breaks my heart. We're going to kill good people along the way, not just the bad ones. How do you suppose that makes me feel? I'm not without emotion. This is about protecting our way of life. Even if you're not big and strong, you can make a contribution to our cause. My plan includes deception as well. You weaker ones out there, go about your business as usual. Interact with the enemy. Be courteous. If you see them on the road, give them free access and stay clear. Don't start trouble. I don't want to see you on television, causing a big scene. That's the last thing we need. Be a good neighbor. Pretend you're as clueless as the rest of them as to why their world is collapsing around them."

Another question came from the crowd. "Should we be nicer than usual?"

This irritated Mother. "You must have the mental capacity of a squirrel. Seriously, aren't you listening?"

"You don't have to be nasty. I don't want to screw this up," the voice shouted, shivering, a layer of fresh snow covering his winter coat.

"No, I'm the one who should apologize," said Mother. "I'm sorry for snapping at you. You're not used to this type of violent rhetoric. You come from diverse backgrounds, but this fight unites us all…and with divinity on our side. God would cry if he saw what has become of his Earth."

Two weeks went by, and I scoured every drop of Internet news but couldn't uncover a single story about a threat of global war from a small army in Ohio, or anywhere for that matter. I arrived at the *Lake County Herald News* offices and practiced the beginning of my speech to my editor. Each time

I stopped, realizing the folly. I needed proof. I wanted to return to the woods and search for that woman, the one with the voice that left me transfixed by its beauty and strength. I had tried to figure out her accent, or dialect, find a clue that would reveal her background. Who could fund the massive resources required to launch a battle of this size? I replayed her words over and over in my head. Was there really an army behind her swagger and braggadocio? Part of me still believed her story was crazy, yet I had a gut feeling she was dangerous. She had sucked me into her tangled web, and I needed to see this through.

I scoured through my phone records, searching for her number, but I quickly discovered she had used a private number to contact me. I called my buddy, Mr. Cherry, at the Lake County sheriff's department and asked if he could find out the number for me. He said he'd try but couldn't make any promises. Two days later, I hadn't heard back from him. I sat near my window, staring at the evening sky, watching the snow fall, thinking of her, when my phone rang. The song "Strangers in the Night" played softly, and Sinatra singing at a Las Vegas nightclub jumped to life in front of me. Ol' Blues Eyes was back. All incoming private calls now played this song. I answered and identified her unique voice immediately.

"I was thinking about you this very moment and you called. Your number comes up as private, so I didn't have a way to reach you."

Mother said, "Fortunate timing, don't you think? Are you ready to make headlines?"

"And what exactly will I say? There's a threat out there without a name or a face, or a motive?"

"I'm quite motivated, thank you very much."

"Let me rephrase. I think you're a crackpot. Do you think I'm a fool?"

"I read your last article on fossil fuel replacements," she said. "You're already making a fool of yourself quite easily without my assistance."

"Ouch. Insulting the man you want to help you. Where did you learn your manners?"

"His name was Father T."

I seized the moment to gather valuable clues. "Father William Thomas?" I exclaimed. "Was he the pastor of your church? I go to St. Ann's Church on Cedar Road. I studied under Father Thomas when I was a kid at Cleveland Heights High School. Is that the guy? The church is right down the street from me. I could meet your there in twenty minutes."

She clearly wanted no part of explaining her past and quickly changed the subject. "I'm in the middle of the Allegheny Forest tonight. I could meet you tomorrow. Noon? Same place?"

"The weather is supposed to get really nasty," I told her. "I don't have snow tires, and we're expecting six to eight inches of snow and plummeting temperatures. How about we set up our next meeting once the storm passes?"

Mother scoffed. "Don't be a worrywart. The roads will be fine."

"Do you work for the Ohio Department of Transportation?"

"You're the reporter," she said. "You figure it out. See you tomorrow at noon." *Click.*

The next day I drove to our clandestine meeting spot. The snowfall for the area fell short of expectations, but even three inches of the white stuff made chugging through the unpaved walkways of Blossom a challenge.

Mother chuckled at my perspiration. "Quite a cardiovascular test, huh?"

"Still hiding from view? What's your real name again?"

"Nice try, rookie. 'Mother' is good enough at this juncture. When we're at the precipice of victory, you'll see me. I promise. But today I'm upset with you. You haven't written a word about what's happening."

"I've decided not to," I told her. "Nobody will trust me unless I have proof. And you're not giving me any. The story lies dormant until I can report facts, not rumors."

"Your paper barely covered the increased traffic at the neighborhood health clinic. That's the tip of the iceberg. You should look deeper into that."

"Duly noted. Thanks for the scoop," I said. "I'm not printing your story. Find another stooge for your amusement. For some strange reason, I can't get you out of my mind and felt compelled to drive all the way here to say that to your face."

"I appreciate the candor and the effort, Mr. Parker. I expected that. I'm prepared to make you another offer."

"I'm listening."

"I want you to keep a log of your journey. Envision yourself as a war correspondent for your side."

I broke in, "My side?"

"You heard me. Yes, your side. The losing side, like the United States in Vietnam. You're too young to recall Walter Cronkite telling millions of Americans the war was unwinnable."

I couldn't believe she had referenced my news hero, Cronkite. It had to be more than blind luck to make that connection to a news report from 1968. How did this woman know of my admiration for the former television anchor from so long ago?

"I know all about what Cronkite said," I retorted. "You don't have to teach me about the lessons of Vietnam and his stellar reporting. If I decided to keep track of your crusade and the story isn't published, what's the point?"

Without hesitation, she said, "For posterity. There must be a written record of how it happened. I admire your style of writing, and you're a deeply committed tree hugger. Isn't that the phrase?"

"That's an old saying. That's an expression used to insult people who care more about the environment than the portfolios of Wall Street billionaires."

"Now you sound like you're feeling the Bern."

I said, "Another old saying. From what my dad told me, he could have won if the Democrats had played fair. They got their chosen candidate and got trumped instead."

"Nice play on words, Mr. Parker. Are you interested in the job or not?"

"What does it pay?"

"Nothing," she said. "But you can have the movie rights."

"Perfect!"

We talked for two more hours. I never did see her face. The things she told me blew my mind. She relayed details of ecological disasters that governments around the world had kept from the media to protect large corporations from lawsuits. I wrote everything down, made notes, and promised to keep a journal as events transpired. When I was ready to leave, I asked her, "When is this going to start? How will I know when it's over? You promised I would see you when that happens. And what should I do with my report?"

"The battle has already started," she explained. "I can assure you it's begun and irreversible. People will read your report when the chaos is over. You'll meet me soon enough."

February 18, 2047

I haven't written in a while. There's a full notebook in my backpack in case I need to scramble out of here. I've documented all the latest news releases. It's getting bad out there, and I'm worried. Who wouldn't be? The climate-change deniers turned silent in full retreat. The continued warming of the planet has had far reaching consequences. As sea levels inched higher, small islands in the Pacific Ocean vanished, swept under by rising waters. It'll take hundreds of years for the planet to cool and those islands to reemerge. They're likely gone forever. Scientists predicted we'd have until the year 2100 to worry about a global disaster. Something triggered an exponential rise in global temperatures this year. That came on the heels of a bigger problem: CO_2 levels in the atmosphere rose to record-breaking highs. Scientists said the dramatic shift was due to increased ocean acidification and the sudden die-off of millions of trees.

Anyone who discovers my journals can search the web, if that still exists, and read detailed reports on my website about how increased acidity in the oceans effects air quality. All my notes are there, and the web address is in the zippered pocket of this bag. Here's the quick version if books and the Internet fall victim to this nightmare: as CO_2 in the ocean increases, plankton dies. Plankton provides oxygen. Remember oxygen? That's the stuff we're severely lacking. That's a real simple version of an extremely complicated problem.

Most people thought all our oxygen came from trees. But half of it, depending on which study you pull off the shelf, comes from those squiggly dudes in the ocean. Okay, stranger, are you still with me? We're losing oxygen from the ocean. Thank God, we have the trees to protect our air supply. Wait, sorry, the trees are dying too. Nobody knows why. I remember talking to a forest ranger a few years ago. He said there were three trillion trees in the world. That's trillion with a "t." Environmentalists pushed to prohibit deforestation. What's the big deal if we lose a billion trees to make paper and pencils, and houses, and lots of other stuff if we have three trillion in reserve? It was a big deal for those who lived in those areas. Humans have a way of seeing problems through the narrow lens of their own houses or cities. Hardships in Brazil or China don't change lives in Ohio. Of course, in the long run, they do. But who lives long enough to see it happen? Last week the Armed Forces Radio Network said the only place trees aren't dying is New Zealand. Go figure, right? So, what's killing the trees? That's the rub. We don't have a clue, and more important, we don't know how to stop it. If this keeps up, we're done. Kaput. Finished.

It's already "killing season" for folks with respiratory ailments. Hospitals are full of patients suffering from asthma, COPD, and bronchitis. One old geezer dies, and before the staff can change the sheets, another person is ready to lie down and take his place. I lost my grandfather and grandmother within a week. They smoked cigarettes their entire adult lives; their lungs were toast. All the oxygen in the world wouldn't sustain them for long. The "Atomic 8," as it came to be known, killed them in a matter of days. Oxygen is number eight on the periodic table of elements, and the surgeon general wanted a gimmicky name for this disaster. During a press conference, he blurted, "Lack of atomic number 8 is killing us," and the name stuck. Scientists love naming things. The government stopped shipments of oxygen tanks to hospitals for anyone over the age of fifty. I guess that AARP card doesn't get you any benefits in this situation. No, it gets you a one-way ticket out of this living hell. There's a black market for oxygen right now. Nobody smokes anymore. It's too dangerous, and now, more than ever, it's bad for your long-term survival. The government shut down sales of cigarettes. I never thought that would happen.

I wish I knew when this war of attrition would end. I have to ration my weekly supply of oxygen. Hopefully I'll be strong enough to write again soon.

February 28, 2047

This is all happening so fast. I'm down to my last canister of air. The National Guard won't promise that more deliveries of oxygen tanks are on the way. They say the air is better the closer you get to the poles, but no one will confirm or deny it. The trees, for the most part, are dead. I heard they're still alive in New Zealand, though. Their government sealed off the borders and won't let anyone enter the country, not even President Burke. Asshole, serves him right. Ten billion dollars in his bank vault, and he'd trade it all for a few thousand containers of oxygen or admittance to New Zealand. The freakin' Kiwis have more sheep than humans, and that's the way they want to keep it. They're all living fine. Whatever killed the trees and the oceans bypassed the nice folks in Wellington. Good for them. They never hurt anyone.

March 22, 2047

Let me give you a better picture of what's happening around here. The only safe place is an army resettlement camp. It's too dangerous to live on your own. Two weeks ago, I left Cleveland Heights; I'm now living near Wooster, Ohio. There's five thousand of us sleeping in army barracks. The guy next to me snores like a bear. He says the government wouldn't let him bring his CPAP machine. I'm trading a canister of oxygen to switch spots with a guy named Moses. He's deaf, so the snoring won't bother him. He won't switch for free. Can't say I blame him. Bartering is the new monetary system these days. That and sex. My new friend, Melissa, says I'm an idiot for trading it. She would have traded sex with me for a tank. Tough call, but I figured if I can't stand being awake and witnessing what has become of the world, I might as well enjoy a few hours of sleep before I die. In my dreams I breathe clean air. Most of the people here are kids, barely out of high school. The president signed an executive order that allowed entry into the camp for people who are under the age of thirty and in good health. When I was nineteen, I bought a fake driver's license that said I was twenty-two. I got it to purchase booze. My real age is thirty-one, and I'd be dead without it. I might die in a few more weeks anyway. I've heard what's happening around the globe. My editor always told me to say it in as few words as possible. This ought to sum it up succinctly: death and destruction.

Marauding groups of thugs are killing for sport, raping, looting, and scavenging for medicine. Most of them come from New York, not Mexico. Those good people from New York are desperate. They weren't killers a year ago. They worked at banks or taught ninth-grade music class or labored in a steel mill. They were honest, upstanding citizens taking care of their families. Once law and order broke down, look out, mild-mannered people lost their sense of humanity when faced with the death of their children or spouse. I'm glad I don't have either, because I'm barely hanging on, and there's no way I could take care of anyone else. I've seen parents drop their kids off here and drive away. They might never see them again. It's heartbreaking. They're calling us for our weekly shower. I'm tired and need to rest.

April 1, 2047

I'm thinking this is the end for me. Our entire encampment has run out of oxygen canisters. The air smells terrible, and we spend our nights foraging for food. We've come across a few animals, but most of them are dead or diseased. They have to breathe too. Whenever we get a strong southerly breeze, there's hope for a minute that the wind will bring fresh air, but it doesn't. It's worse when it rains, which doesn't happen much anymore. I always thought of myself as a smart guy, but I didn't understand the science of how trees help create rain. One of the men at the camp is a chemistry professor from the College of Wooster. He rigged a machine that cleans rainwater. He also has a few air scrubbers, like the ones from that old movie *Apollo 13*. You should look that movie up. "Houston, we have a problem." I love that line. Those air cleaners help, and if we could build more of them, we might survive until the planet rights itself. We're miles from any town, and it's too dangerous to travel to look for supplies. We sent out a search party last week, but they never came back; they're probably dead.

I fell down yesterday and busted up my knee pretty bad. The one doctor we have here came to see me, patched me up as best he could. He said I'll probably get an infection because he doesn't have enough medicine to kill all the germs running through my body, and the poor air quality is preventing my body from healing at an optimum pace. Nice phrase, Doc: "optimum pace." He won't say it, but I know he wants to tell me I'm dying because I was a klutz who fell down and hurt my knee. What a stupid way to die.

April 26, 2047

Melissa told me it's Arbor Day. If that isn't the biggest, sickest joke of all time, I don't know what is. There's no more living trees. Not around here at least. There's lot of dead wood we can burn to stay warm, but fire consumes what little oxygen remains. How the hell do you celebrate Arbor Day without any trees?

My leg is infected, and there was talk of cutting it off above the knee. I told them to forget that idea immediately. If this is the end, so be it. If there's a heaven, I'm heading there with two legs, not one and a half.

I saw my mystery woman from the woods. I was dreaming, but I swear it felt real. I knew the voice right away. She said, "Spencer Parker, I see you've kept up with your writing. That's good. I'm proud of you. Someone will find your journals and retell the story of how mankind's reign on Earth came to an end."

I said, "I want to see the face that goes with your exquisite voice."

She told me I'd see it tonight. I hope she's right. I need closure. In my dream, I managed to see an outline of her face and body. It glowed with an opalescent splendor. It radiated warmth and made me feel loved. That was the worst part of what happened to mankind. All the love vanished from the world. It got sucked out along with the air. I asked her how she had kicked our butt without firing a single shot. She told me she forced the trees to commit suicide. Who knew trees could do that? She said they accepted their fate, even the tall ones in the back of the wooded area where we first met. They shut down their intake of water and stopped processing CO_2 from the air. They communicated with one another through their vast network of roots that ran from coast to coast and beneath the oceans. She's restocking the planet with new trees as I write these words. Eventually those seedlings will replenish the oxygen as they grow. Unfortunately, it won't happen quickly enough to save most of mankind.

Plankton is growing in the oceans again, aiding in the restoration of the atmosphere. She said nature is reclaiming Earth. She found no pleasure in our near extinction. She insisted I write that. Those were her words, not mine. Mankind is no longer at the top of the food chain. She left a few pockets of humanity here and there, scattered around the globe. Perhaps, given the knowledge of what happened, and from reading my chronicles, those who remain will respect the sanctity of all God's creatures and never forget what transpired.

I'm pretty sleepy now. I can't feel my leg, and my lungs are weak. Breathing is a difficult chore. I've written enough. I hope I see Mother's face soon. And that's the way it is.

The Outcast Gem

Tanja Rohini Bisgaard

Astrid swore through clenched teeth as she examined the circuit board. It had burned out again. She had lost track of the number of times she had replaced it. Inspecting every inch of the Carbon Extractor Pro, version who-could-remember-by-now, she checked for additional damage along its sleek design. A setback like this could ruin everything. Just the thought of it brought tiny droplets to her upper lip.

"I think if you replaced that wire over there—"

"Shut up!" Astrid snapped.

She looked over the machine at Ingrid, who had entered the lab without making a sound. The pressure on her molars built as she gritted her teeth in an attempt to control her temper. Today, of all days, she didn't need useless comments from her outcast twin sister.

Ingrid closed her mouth in a dramatic gesture, making her look like a fish. Her shaved head made her mouth seem bigger. She rattled something that sounded like a handful of stones in her pocket as she turned away from Astrid and faced the window.

"Look, I'm sorry," Astrid said. "But you know how important this work is to me. I've been trying to figure this out for two years, and I don't seem to be getting anywhere!"

Astrid continued to scrutinize the machine: every surface, every wire, every detail on the control panel. The smell of burnt metal still lingered in her nostrils.

"Damn!" She slammed her hands on the table in front of her, creating a prickly sensation that travelled up her arms almost instantaneously.

"What happened?" Ingrid turned around, her eyebrows raised, igniting even more irritation in Astrid. "What's wrong?" she asked again.

"The flames from the circuit board melted part of the solar panel." Astrid pointed to the machine.

Ingrid walked over to her sister, her eyebrows still raised, making Astrid feel like she had just failed her most important exam in microelectronics. She felt as though the top of her head was glowing, a sensation that spread downward until her cheeks started to burn.

"But that's easy enough to replace," Ingrid said casually, running a finger over the crumpled surface that had been a smooth ebony panel minutes earlier.

"That's not the problem."

"What is then?"

"The lab director won't let me buy any more."

"Why?"

"They're too expensive." Astrid rubbed her eyes. The last thing she needed was to participate in an inquisition conducted by her sister.

"So why don't you use the other type of solar panels, the ones that are cheaper?"

"They don't work as well. Believe me, I've tried. The ones with tellurium are the best."

"I thought you were good at convincing people to let you do stuff," Ingrid said. Her raised eyebrows had now turned into a smirk.

Astrid took a deep breath and chose to ignore her.

"That machine's not going to make a difference anyway," Ingrid continued dryly.

"What do you mean?" Tiny pearls of sweat formed on Astrid's forehead. They'd had this conversation numerous times. Sometimes she wondered if her sister knew something she wasn't telling her. Ingrid had shown up at the Climate Adaptation Lab almost once a week during the last month. Each time using a new fake ID, appearing in Astrid's workspace like a ghost.

"Do you really think that one little device you're making will help us?"

"Yes, I do," Astrid replied. "If we can figure out how to get this machine to work, we can start extracting CO2 from the atmosphere and reduce global warming. But obviously we'll need many of them. All over the world."

Ingrid's eyes grew darker. "But you do know that even if you start extracting CO2 from the atmosphere now, it'll take decades, or maybe even centuries, before the temperature on Earth will be reduced." Ingrid's face grew somber as she turned to look out the window at the myriad of lab buildings connected by newly built bridges over recently formed canals.

"Yes, of course I know." Astrid sighed and put a hand on Ingrid's shoulder. "But I do believe I can make a difference with this machine. Imagine if I could get all that water out there to turn into glaciers again."

Ingrid's mouth formed a crooked grin. "Yeah, right! I'd like to see you figure that out. I think Copenhagen is stuck with all these canals for a while. And we're stuck with being the Isles of Denmark, too."

"Maybe. But it doesn't have to be like that forever."

The sisters stared out the window at the June snowflakes slowly making their way into the water. It wasn't an unusual sight this time of year. If the country's residents wanted to feel the sun on their skin, they either had to visit a tanning booth or travel toward the equator.

"No, I know," Ingrid said. "Do you remember when we were kids and we could go swimming in the sea?"

Astrid nodded, reluctantly letting her thoughts take her back. "But even if the Gulf Stream can bring some warmer waters up here again, I wouldn't want to bathe in that water!" She gestured toward the stagnant greenish canal right in front of the window. "Some say it's lethal if it gets on your skin."

Ingrid shrugged. "Surely someone will figure out how to do something useful with those toxic algae soon." She tapped a finger on the windowpane and straightened her back. "But you know, maybe I could help you repair that machine you're working on," she said, and turned a hopeful face toward Astrid. "And then the two of us together can solve the world's problem. After all, Dad named us after two of the most famous Danish climate scientists."

"Yeah, of the last century! Listen to our names: Astrid and Ingrid. We don't sound like we're living in 2047!" Astrid exclaimed. "And anyway, I hate to point out the obvious, but I'm the only real scientist here."

"No, you don't need to point out the obvious," Ingrid muttered. "Hardly anyone even knows I exist."

The invisible wall between them grew higher. Astrid always felt guilty when her sister brought this up, even though it had nothing to do with her. Their parents had made the decision a long time ago. The one-child policy in the European Republic of Independent Nations had given only

Astrid the opportunity to get an education. Their mother had refused to keep just one of the fetuses when she discovered she was pregnant with twins. And when she gave birth, the doctor kindly pretended he had seen only one baby. But when Astrid and her sister turned four, their parents had to make an impossible choice regarding whom to send to school. The consequence was that Ingrid had to live as a ghost her entire life.

As a child, Astrid had been ashamed of having a sister who couldn't be seen in public. In the beginning, her parents wouldn't allow her to bring any friends home after school. As a result, Ingrid became an impediment to Astrid's social life. And as a family, they were rarely able to do anything together outside of the compound where they lived. Even though most of their neighbors had accepted the illegal child living next door, some of them whispered in the corners and walked away whenever Astrid and her twin approached. And finding friends to play with proved hard for Astrid whenever Ingrid was around. Eventually their parents gave in and allowed a few of her closest friends to come over.

At first, Ingrid hid in her bedroom, having been instructed to be quiet for as long as Astrid had visitors. Later on, however, Ingrid refused to remain a secret and entered Astrid's room while other girls were there. There was no going back after that. The twins' mother made Astrid's friends swear not to say anything about Ingrid. Not even to their own parents.

Quickly changing the subject, Astrid said, "But you're still pretty intelligent. Sometimes I wonder if you're as clever as I am!"

Ingrid's eyes flashed as the careless comment slipped from her sister's lips. "Well, you take pretty good notes, Astrid. And honestly, the stuff you learned at university isn't really that complicated—or even the stuff you're doing here." She nodded toward Astrid's desk as she put her hand in her pocket and rattled what she was concealing again, all the while giving her twin sister a rebellious look.

Astrid knew perfectly well that Ingrid was as intelligent as she was. Their father had insisted on hiring a private tutor, who spent as much time teaching Ingrid as Astrid spent at school. Ingrid could have easily passed all the exams Astrid did. On several occasions, Astrid had even gotten help from Ingrid when she was studying for her tests. Without her, Astrid's grades probably wouldn't have been good enough for her to get the PhD she was about to complete.

Astrid walked back to the machine and began extracting the damaged circuit board. If she could make this device work, her name would be on the lips of every climate scientist in the world. And maybe even on everyone else's lips—and in the newspapers, on TV, and online. Not to mention all the articles she would be writing for the most renowned journals.

"Why are you here anyway?" Astrid asked Ingrid, not taking her eyes off the burnt wires. If she was going to convince the director to let her buy those solar panels, she'd better make sure they were safe from becoming incinerated again. "You've come to the lab so many times over the past month."

Ingrid didn't reply, so Astrid decided on a different approach to soften her up.

60

"How are things with you? Mum and Dad said you haven't been home to visit them for weeks. Have you got a place to sleep? And do you get enough to eat?" Astrid bit her lip; she sounded too much like their mother.

"You really have no idea, do you?" Ingrid replied. "All this time, and you've never wondered how I survive? Well, I'll tell you. I have plenty of Eurobits to buy food and pay my bills. Without getting help from anyone."

Astrid looked up and felt her face turn red. Ingrid was right—she had no idea how her sister got by, but honestly, she didn't really care that much. She spent most of her time in the lab, working on this machine. Doing so was the only way to make sure she was the first one in the world to make a breakthrough with carbon-extraction technology. And anyway, she knew Ingrid was resourceful. She would be fine.

"So you live in a house?"

Ingrid nodded.

"And you buy your own food? And clothes?"

Ingrid nodded again. "You mean you didn't even notice the jacket I have on?"

Astrid inspected it. She wasn't particularly interested in the new high-tech clothing that was flooding the market these days. Clothes that could last forever and never needed to be washed, saving the consumer money and protecting the environment. Clothes that self-regulated the temperature a person felt when wearing the garment, making the need for seasonal fashion obsolete. Clothes that monitored everything imaginable: pulse rate, blood pressure, indoor and outdoor temperatures. Some items of clothing even picked up signals from people in the vicinity, to inform wearers if there was a stressed or calm atmosphere in the room they were about to enter. And those were just a few of the new features Astrid saw when she looked through the daily news video bulletins. She wondered what Ingrid's jacket could do. But she didn't ask.

"But how do you pay for all those things?" she asked instead.

Ingrid pulled her hand out of her pocket and extended it. Astrid leaned over the worktable to examine the tiny objects she was holding. They looked like the pebbles they'd found when they were young and spent their holidays in the Swedish mountains.

"What are they?"

"Diamonds." Ingrid opened her backpack, took out a small fern-colored velvet bag, and poured its contents onto the worktable. "And these I just picked up today from my gemologist. Real beauties, once they've been cut and polished, aren't they?"

Astrid examined the perfectly cut stones filtering the sharp lab light like tiny prisms, allowing them to sparkle in all the colors of the rainbow. "Where do you find them? I thought most of the diamond mines were flooded years ago."

"I've created a machine that can make them."

"Oh, I see. Well, there are several ways of making diamonds," Astrid said indifferently. "But you need a license for that. How do you sell them?"

Ingrid shrugged as she put the diamonds back in her bag.

Astrid realized she wouldn't get an answer. "Which method are you using?" she continued.

"A new method. Based on your notes."

Astrid shot her a surprised look. "What do you mean?"

Ingrid smiled wryly. "You're the scientist. You mean you can't figure it out?"

Astrid racked her brain, her thoughts suddenly jumbled. She had never built a machine to make diamonds. She hated when her sister tried to outsmart her like this. Particularly when she succeeded at it.

"I really can't think of any of the machines I've built that would give you stones like that."

"Really?"

"Really." Astrid took a deep breath and sighed. She could no longer be bothered playing this game. "Well, tell me if you want, but I've got work to do. So please leave." She picked up a tiny pair of tweezers and placed the toasted circuit board in front of her, making sure to look busy.

"All right, I'll show you." Ingrid's voice carried throughout the room. "But you'll have to come with me."

"Why?"

"Because if I tell you, you won't believe me."

Astrid clenched her fists before she looked up to face her sister. "You'd better not be stringing me along. I've got so much work to do, and I really don't fancy wasting my time looking at some useless invention of yours."

"I don't think you'll find it useless…quite the contrary. You'll like the side effects," Ingrid replied calmly, and walked toward the door with confident steps. "Are you coming?"

They exited the high-security lab through a body scanner before using their IDs to walk through the monitor gates. As Ingrid held her wrist over the chip reader, Astrid saw the name Jill Winter displayed for a split second. She had no idea how her sister had been able to insert an approved ID nano chip into herself and, in addition, constantly change her name and all the other information that was stored on the chip.

Astrid followed Ingrid to the aerial parking garage where her sister had left the two-person transport drone. It seemed to be the newest model in the entire parking lot, and the only decacopter. Ingrid disabled the wireless battery charger by tapping a blue panel on the ground with the tip of her shoe.

"Climb in, and I'll take you to see my home," Ingrid said, grinning as she slid the door open for her sister.

"I don't really care about seeing your place. If I did, I would've visited you ages ago. I'm only coming along because you promised me whatever you've made would be interesting to me."

Astrid sat down on a white seat that looked like leather. She guessed it was made of mushroom skin or something similar. No one could get a hold of real leather anymore; there weren't enough animals for that. She clandestinely slid her fingers over the soft surface before crossing her arms demonstratively and leaning back in the comfortable seat.

Ingrid didn't respond as she switched on the engine and the self-driving electric transport drone lifted vertically in the air, before she entered the coordinates of their destination and they headed toward the southern part of the city. Below them the center of Copenhagen stretched toward the sky, giving them a view of the many building projects approved by the government: the addition of extra floors to existing buildings or the construction of annexes to serve as individual quays so office buildings could have direct access to the canals and the water taxis. The older generation often used the name New Venice when they spoke of the city. Astrid had heard about the many canals in the old Italian town and recalled seeing a photograph of Venice at school, before the water had swallowed it up.

As they flew past the city center and approached the outskirts, the buildings decreased in height, and eventually houses were replaced by a vast undeveloped area composed of ocean-plastic cobblestones defining the man-made coast. Fifteen minutes after takeoff, Ingrid landed the transport drone, and they climbed out onto the wobbly surface.

"Watch your step. They haven't secured these stones for years, and they're loose in some places. Last week I stepped into a hole, and my entire leg fell into the water," Ingrid said, as she headed toward a small house made of carbon fiber, seemingly built too close to the sea. Apprehensively Astrid followed her until they reached the back of the building.

In front of her stood a piece of towering equipment covered with a thin tarp, only displaying the cables as they turned and twisted along the cobblestones toward the sea before finally disappearing into the water.

"Here it is," Ingrid proclaimed, and pulled off the cover. Astrid stared at the large orb in front of them. It looked very similar to the Carbon Extractor Pro in her lab. It was just bigger. A loud thumping coursed through her temples.

"So does it really work?" she asked with a trembling voice.

"Well, after I looked at your notes in the lab one day two years ago—"

"Yes, I got that. I realize you built this based on my notes. But that wasn't my question!"

"All right, yes, it works. I extract carbon from the air and turn the atoms into diamonds."

Trying to ignore her sister's aloof tone, Astrid pointed to a small glass cylinder on the side of the machine. "And what does this do? My notes didn't include this."

"It's a pressure chamber."

Astrid nodded. Of course. But her machine didn't need that because she wasn't making diamonds.

"I didn't really have anywhere to store the carbon I was extracting. So I thought this would be more fun—and definitely more useful."

"But how were you able to get this to work when I can't get my machine to work?" she blurted. Now she sounded really stupid in front of her outcast twin. Astrid took a deep breath to calm her galloping heart. "Switch it on so I can see if you're telling the truth."

Ingrid tapped a yellow panel at the foot of the machine. Drawing electricity from the submerged solar panels, it started up with a low humming noise. The inner blade of the orb rotated, and after a short while, the pressure chamber buzzed. The orb picked up so much speed that it was impossible to tell whether it was moving. A minute later, a sharp clank resounded from the glass cylinder and a small pebble formed inside it. Ingrid opened a lid at the top of the chamber and reached in to retrieve the rough diamond.

"Here, a present from me. Your first gem made from my machine," Ingrid said with a proud look. "And take a deep breath. The air just became a little more invigorating."

Even though Astrid wished she had been the one to make the breakthrough, she couldn't help looking at her sister with admiration. Flashing before her eyes were all the newspaper headings and academic journals describing the machine that would save humanity—they just didn't have her name on it, as she had dreamed.

Ingrid put a hand on Astrid's arm, tearing her out of her reverie. "And the best part is you and I can build loads of these together."

Astrid nodded. Maybe her name could be in all those places after all. Next to her sister's. "I'd be honored to," she said. Astrid slid her hand under Ingrid's arm. "Why don't you show me how you made this machine work?"

Together they walked to Ingrid's workshop at the back of her house.

Dear Henry

David Zetland

May 13, 2047
Visalia, California

Hank walked into the office. It was already hot and he was already tired, even though the sun had only risen a few hours earlier. He looked around at the stacks of boxes, distracted by a fly at the window. The air conditioning was off in this room because it was "no longer essential." He sighed as he sat down at his desk—his great-grandfather's desk actually—and looked at the mostly bare walls. Empty squares showed where decades of photos and trivia had documented his family's life in this area. The only remaining memento was a rough-hewn plank that his distant namesake had nailed to the wall. The plank was carved with the pledge familiar to every Sisson:

WE WILL DEFEND AND BUILD THIS RICH LAND FOR THE BENEFIT OF OUR DESCENDANTS —HENRY H. SISSON (1876)

Hank sipped his coffee and winced as the pinched nerve in his back sent painful tingles from his hips to his ears. The last few years had been stressful, the last few weeks even more so. It wasn't just that the Sisson's were moving for the first time in 180 years. It was the circumstances forcing their departure. He had done his best, as had his father—and yet they had to leave. What had they missed?

The pinch in his consciousness was like the pinch in his back: sporadic, painful, and inexplicable. He sympathized with his nerve, which seemed caught in the same mix of forces, squeezing, twisting, and pulling him in novel, disconcerting ways.

The dust was dangerous and the air too hot. The tanker water smelled bad. Hank's neighbors—the ones who were left—hardly registered in his consciousness. Social visits had dropped to the bare minimum. There hadn't been a wedding in four years. The number of funerals had dropped only because most people had left to die elsewhere.

Hank rubbed his throbbing neck, closed his eyes, and breathed slowly.

The door opened.

"Oh, here you are. Ouch—you look like you've been stung. Old wrestling injury?"

His father walked over and gently touched his son's neck.

"'Morning, Dad. No, I've just got pain up and down my back. Nerves maybe. How are you?"

"I slept well last night, for a change, and I'll tell you about that in a sec. I just wanted to let you know that your mother and I had a chat with Jenny about the baby and our future. She's worried, and she's not from around here, so it took a while to explain how we get things done and what we need to do."

"Thanks. Yeah, I've been telling her, but I think the baby's arrival and our departure have been double-teaming her for a few months. Actually, I guess they've been double-teaming me too, if my back's any guide."

"Yeah, it's got all of us in a bind, doesn't it?"

"Tell me, Dad... How did we get in this position if we've been following the old man's advice?" He pointed to the plank.

"Ahhh, well, that's a long story, I reckon. The way I see it is that it's a story of me and you and everyone else, except nobody was really paying attention to the plot, direction wise."

"But didn't we have a plot?" Hank asked. "A direction? I thought we were supposed to be here for generations. Isn't that what those words mean?"

"Yeah, I know what you're saying, and I was confused too, until last night. I was putting some stuff away and opened the letter box for the first time in a while."

"The letter box? I haven't seen it since I turned sixteen. What did you find?"

"Well," Hank's father said, "I didn't really find anything new or surprising—I just looked back. I read older letters to my dad, granddad, and so on—back to the beginning. It was an interesting read."

"So what did they say? What did you learn?"

"I think you should read them first. I'm curious to hear what you think. The box is over there."

Hank shook his head. "I don't have time right now."

"Don't worry. We have plenty of time until the movers get here—and this might be kinda important, from a pain-relief perspective." He grinned.

Henry Senior (he was really Henry the Sixth, but the family dropped the numbers in daily life) laid a kind hand on his son's shoulder. "Just sit and read for a bit. I'll tell the others I found you." He turned on the old desk fan, pointed it in his son's direction, and left the room.

71

Hank tilted open the box, dumped out a sheaf of papers, and arranged them on the desk. He picked up the oldest one. The ink had turned brown, but the strong, crude letters were clear.

April the 12th, 1880 AD
Visalia Township, California State

Dear Henry,

If you are reading this, then you are 16 and a Man. If I am not around to buy you your first drink, then use the enclosed $5 to buy yourself a few. You'll need them if you are working hard (and goddamn, I hope you are!).

I want to tell you about our Family and give you some Advice.

I was born in 1850 in Yorkshire, England. Our Family was poor. I was the third oldest of ten Bairn—as we called kids over there—and I worked on our Farm from the day I could carry a bucket. We usually had enough food. I learned letters and maths at School until I joined the Factory at age eleven.

When I was sixteen, we had a Bad Year: rains ruined the harvest before it could dry, Mum and the new Bairn died of the grippe, and my older Brother broke his leg when his horse slipped in the mud. Maybe God wanted to drown us in water, mud, and misery, and we had no defense.

Pa gave me ten quid (about $70 in those days) and told me it was time. "Henry, we are in a tough spot and cannot help you anymore. I have paid Frank Collins to take you with him to New York. It is time to live your Life as a Man."

And what a Life it was! I had many Adventures in New York, but I was still stuck. One day a man came into the Pub where I worked. He said there was FREE LAND in California for anyone who joined him.

Well, I did not need to hear that twice, and I spent half my Savings taking one of the first trains across the Continent. About a month later, I arrived here in Visalia to find that my FREE LAND was flooded most of the year, while Tulare Lake was "wet" (as we used to say).

But we were determined, and the twenty-five of us—we called ourselves the "Duck Farmers"—worked to dam, drain, and divert the Water FROM our Land when it was wet and put it ONTO our Land when it was dry. Over the years, we drained more land and harvested more from this rich Soil.

We've been here about ten years now and Life is better. Tulare Lake has been mostly tamed—she only overflows one year in five—and yields are higher. We have four churches and two schools. The Harvest Festival lasts two days!

A few years ago, I built a Home for me and your Mother. Our first Bairn died, but you've made it past your second year. I am writing to you in case I am not around when you become a Man.

Son, you come from good people of humble origins. Your Granddad was a good Man, but Poverty killed his wife and Debt broke his Family. I have done my best to build a Future for you that you can grow and pass on.

Remember! This Land is for your Sons. Do not gamble. Do not trade tomorrow's Security for today's pleasure. Take care of the Land, and the Land will take care of you.

Your father,
Henry Hugh Sisson, Sr.

[Scrawled below was "Father died in 1908 when a horse threw him off on the way to church."]

Hank sat back and looked around him, his head spinning with images of wet English fields, factories churning out smoke, and a sixteen-year old passing from the land of Dickens to the land of Twain. He wondered what the first Henry was thinking when he arrived to find a lake slowly creeping up to swallow "his" land.

The next letter was written in a fine hand on good paper.

November 12, 1900
Visalia

Dear Henry,

Grandfather reminded me today that I should write you a letter, as you have made it through the first few months without any trouble.

As you will no doubt hear, our life here revolves around the harvest seasons more than the rainy season, and we have had a good year so far. Your grandfather came here over thirty years ago from England and found a land that varied between wet and very wet. It took him and his neighbors fifteen years to get the floods under control, but the past fifteen years have been good. We have a wet spring now and then, but the land has given us bigger harvests and a stronger community.

I was born during one of the last "great floods," as they call them around here. The combination of heavy snowmelt and spring rains nearly brought the water up the steps of the house, and the lower fields were entirely underwater. We almost lost a wagon, but Mr. Vail caught it in his boat and hauled in the biggest catch ever seen in our lake! Those floods are no more, as our dikes and dams hold the water back and we flood our fields whenever we want from wells that are so prolific that they sometimes pump themselves. Most of the lakebed is now farmed because it has such good *soil. Our "lower lower" field used to lie under fifteen feet of water.*

So that is the world you have joined, and I am fairly sure your life will be even better than mine. Our farm and your grandfather's hard work meant that I—and your five uncles and aunts— learned at school, ate well, and received new outfits every other year. We also contribute to the community by hosting barn dances and Harvest Week. Your grandfather has discovered God (much to Grandma's delight), and he often helps down at the church. The new railroad has helped us ship oranges to the city. We're booming!

Grandfather's vision of building this rich land is really paying off for you. Make sure you build for the next generations!

Your loving father,
Henry Hugh Sisson, Jr.

Smiling, Hank put the letter down. He wished he could have met Henry the second, if only to have a beer with his cheerful forebear.

The next letter was typed as if it came from the central office.

76

December 10, 1920
Sisson & Sons, Incorporated
Visalia, California

Dear Henry—

Welcome to the farm! It's been a great year, what with your arrival six months ago and the absolutely fantastic season. We got exceptional yields on the new strain of cotton growing in Lower 2, and we harvested a record tonnage of oranges. Our decision to buy the cotton baler and install the orange-sorting equipment worked out exceptionally well!

Now perhaps you don't realize how important this news is at your tender age, but you surely will appreciate a year like this as you grow up on the Sisson & Sons spread. In fact, this is the best set of years I can remember in my lifetime. (Your granddad seems to think 1905 was good, but the Great War has tinted those years before Ralph—my brother and his second son—died.)

Now, to the point—and in a hurry, as time is short. You're reading this letter because you've reached age sixteen and, as we say, turned a man. Congratulations and have a drink—with me and your granddad—before you get to work.

Sisson & Sons is now one of the larger and more successful farms in the area. We have two professional managers (one for irrigation, one for production), about a dozen full-time employees, and a massive increase in manpower for the cotton and harvest seasons. All these people take time to manage, and I've been helping your granddad for about five years now. The hours are long in summer and short in winter, but it's always important to use your head! We have an amazing operation here that has been built up over several generations, and you'll be part of it.

I'm not sure what's going to happen in the future, but I am sure we can better combine water and land, man and machine to produce the fruit and fiber that will make our family—and our community—prosper!

Your father,
Henry Hugh Sisson III

Hank looked out the window, slightly embarrassed at his young forefather's enthusiasm on the eve of an agricultural depression that would ruin many farms in the 1920s. He didn't dwell on that too long, though, as the next letter— clearly typed in haste—showed that the family had made it through a few tough decades.

13-06-48
Visalia

Henry—

It's your dad here, ~~writing~~ typing you a few notes in the middle of a very busy year for me— and a very special year for you!

Although your birth wasn't the easiest, your mom and the doctors did a bang-up job of pulling you out of one water bubble and into another. Hahaha.

Okay, now seriously, I must get to the point,

78

but it's nearly 10 p.m. and I've had just a drink or tow. DId I tell you that it's been crazy? And how!

Here's the quick version. Everything was going fine here until the Japanese attack on Pearl Harbor tore apart our community. Granddad had a heart attack that day and seemed to be doing better until the local rednecks took the Nakagawa and Tachibana families to the Fairgrounds, where they were held as ENEMY NATIONALS. Idiots! Granddad's heart ~~failed~~ couldn't take the blow of losing his best managers and dear friends of thirty years. That month was hell.

My younger brother, Paul, and I enlisted of course. We volunteered to go to England to defend "Ye Olde Homeland" against the Krauts. We were assigned to different logistics squads, but we both survived. I guess a few years of running three harvesters, two balers, and fifty men had given us some useful skills!

Dad kept the farm wroking pretty well, all things considered, until we got back in 1946. Paul went off to college, but I got back to work. My only ~~sewvenirs~~ souvenirs (damn Frog talk) are two service medals, a German helmet, a scar above my eye from a "discussion concerning a lady," and ONE DESK, SURPLUS from the local recruiting center.

I sure hope you don't have to fight a war, son. It's just a terrible way to blow up years of hard work!

Speaking of hard work...the farm is going great guns! We're waiting for the big canal to bring water down here from Northern CA, where there's so much that they let it flow into the ocean! The wells were dropping before the war, but now they're really dropping as everyone gets back to business.

Luckily, we can afford the deeper wells and bigger pumps until the new water arrives. Your granddad used to say this was the best growing land in the country. He was right, but you need water!

So that's my story, son. Grow fast, grow strong, and let's grow some cotton!

Your dad,
~~Hank~~ Henry Hugh Sisson IV

Hank picked up the next letter. It was typed on paper that already had been used on one side.

Sept. 15, 1970
Visalia, California

Dear Henry,

If you're reading this, congratulations on reaching sixteen! The world—our world—has been all topsy-turvy for the past few years. There's been a war that's upset a lot of people—hippies and patriots alike. There's been unrest in the cities over race and poverty, and there's even been unrest in our area, as Chavez and the farmworkers have organized to protest working conditions. I have no idea how all this is going to work out, but "the times REALLY are a changin'!"

The world I grew up in is the same in some ways but different in others. Hippies say we need to stop using the chemicals we've used for decades. I can see their point when it comes to fruit, maybe, but cotton is different. I don't think hippies have seen how bugs can mess a crop, let alone how chemicals and fertilizers boost yields. You'll need a university degree to work in this world, but I'm not sure if you'll need to study law, chemistry, business—or all three!

Although Dad is quite suspicious of "them damned hippies," I can see their point. Since I was born, the Corps has dammed the Kern, Kings, and Tule and Kaweah rivers, which used to flow down our way. Now all that water is stored behind dams and sent on the farmers' schedules, not the schedules of nature or the fish. I've noticed fewer birds and frogs compared to when I was a kid. That's probably a bad sign.

The good news is that all these dams and canals have increased our water supply and strengthened our business. The State Water Project has finally started to deliver water that was promised from before I was born! Too bad it's on the other side of the Valley!

Anyway, I'm pretty sure we'll do fine—you, me, and your mom. I wasn't too sure about marrying so young, but Dad said we had a good foundation here, and your mom wanted a big farm family (!). She says you've carried easily, so maybe she'll get her way. We've gotta hang together while the world around us falls apart!

Your dad <=== I still get a shiver when I
read this!
Henry Hugh Sisson V

The next letter was familiar. Hank had read it sixteen
years earlier...

Jan. 21, 2005
Visalia

Dear Henry,

Well, it's been a long wait for me to write this
letter, but "life is complicated" sometimes! By your
age now, you will have discovered girls but not
necessarily all the complications that come with
girls. Let's have a beer after you read this, and I'll
explain your dad's "complicated" youth :)

So, to the farm—and the point of our lives, loves,
and passions. The farm is doing okay from a
financial perspective. We own the local pistachio
processor and still get good orange yields on the
upper field, but we've had to switch to different
strains of hay on Lower and Lower 2 to deal with
the salt in the soil. We've also been experimenting
on different watering schedules (you'll definitely be
a water master by sixteen!), as the water table is
now over eight hundred feet below the surface.
Your great-granddad used to gripe about water at
fifteen feet. Ha!

82

Along with this letter, I'm putting $5,000 in our savings account. That's because you're going to college when you get older. I took a law degree after my university studies in agricultural enterprise management, and I can tell you a law degree is necessary to defend the farm against environmentalists, argue groundwater at the irrigation office, and file for relief when salt kills an orchard. I sure hope we can afford to educate you to defend this farm, but maybe it would be worth paying a few lobbyists to divert some of this heat!

The good news is that we have the political and financial strength to keep the farm going and the technology (we just upgraded the air and water filters!) to keep you and your mom happy with "country living." :)

XOX,
Papa (aka Henry Hugh Sisson VI!)

Hank set the paper down and looked at his hands. He took a sip of cold coffee and leaned back, staring at the plank on the wall: WE WILL DEFEND AND BUILD THIS RICH LAND...

He remembered the numbers from his father's letter—eight hundred feet and $5,000 from when he was sixteen. At the time, they had assumed they could get by with drip irrigation and salt-tolerant plants, but the water had disappeared at 2,500 feet, and the closest supply, from fifteen miles away, needed to be desalted, even for the Robusta greens. Without water, there wasn't much of a chance that he'd earn back the $200,000 he'd paid for college and two master's degrees, but he needed to find a way. His son was coming.

In the past, the way had been obvious: "Use the land to repay your debts, live comfortably, and build a future for your children," but that option was gone. For over 180 years, the Sissons had built their farm business for the next generation, but that gift, that birthright, had vanished.

His brain was torn between anger, regret, and fatigue. *Fuck.*

He looked back at the plank. DEFEND stared back at him. He went to the bottom of the pile of letters and read, "God wanted to drown us in water, mud, and misery, and we had no defense."

Their defense against the dryness, dust, and heat was drained and dammed and gone, by their own hands.

He tore a piece of paper off a notepad and grabbed a pen.

May 13, 2047

Sisson & Sons Farm

Dear Hank,

This is a cruel letter to write, but our family is honest, and life must be faced in all its glory and tragedy.

You were born at a difficult time for our family. We have farmed and protected this land for nearly two centuries, but now the land is poisoned, the air hot and foul, and the water gone.

I was born here, as were you, but now we have to leave. The farm has failed us, the Earth has failed us, and our neighbors have failed us, so we need to start new lives in new places. It's as if our family is returning to the beginning of a cycle that started nearly two hundred years ago with the birth of the first Henry H. Sisson. This time, it's your turn to begin the cycle.

I'll never forget this day, this loss, and the end of the dreams imagined by so many generations of Sissons. We've kept this name, and this farm, for a reason—for pride of work, pride of place, and pride of people—but now we have to leave. Son, I want you to remember this: it doesn't pay to sacrifice today for payback tomorrow if tomorrow never comes.

I sure hope you grow up in our new home with an appreciation for all that we tried—and will try to do—for you, but don't forget that you're going to have to take care of yourself in this world. Sometimes life just isn't fair, but life also goes on, and those who work hard to seize opportunity can build a better life for themselves and their descendants.

Love you, my boy. We'll make it.
Henry...Goddamn Right...Hugh Sisson VII

Endnote: Although the characters in this story are fictitious, most of the dates, events, and activities are based on the history of Tulare County, which is named after the tule grasses that once grew in the wetlands of California's Central Valley. Tulare Lake, at one time the largest freshwater lake west of the Mississippi, has been dry since 1899, but the old lakebed sometimes floods after heavy rains. In 2008, Visalia was named the fourth most polluted city in the United States due to "inversion layers" that keep high concentrations of particulate pollutants in the air. The author believes the events and conditions he describes in the year 2047 are more probable than not.

NuVenture™ TEMPO-L: A QuickStart Guide

Isaac Yuen

Congratulations on purchasing the NuVenture™ TEMPO-L, ChronoCorp's best-selling, highest-rated, economy-class time machine! Whether you're seeking the latest thrills or the next great family-friendly vacation, the TEMPO-L offers the perfect mix of premium time-jumping experience, no-stress upkeep, and prime fuel efficiency for any budget-conscious traveler. Embark on your first set of adventures today, courtesy of the folks at ChronoCorp!

Before You Start…
Prior to your journey across time and space, please make sure you meet the following criteria to ensure the smooth operation of your NuVenture™ TEMPO-L:
Maintain a minimum clearance of five feet from any other vehicles or structures.
Launch from a level and non-meltable surface (artificial turf not recommended).
Purchase one ChronoCorp ENVIRORAD™ suit per passenger (suits sold separately).
Bring your favorite drinks and snacks for watching history unfold before your eyes!

The NuVenture™ TEMPO-L comfortably seats four and comes equipped with the latest version of TERRAGRIP™ firmware, designed to smooth out any time disturbances you may encounter while keeping you grounded on planet Earth at all times. Worries about drifting off into space or materializing into solid rock are things of the past! All seventh-generation NuVenture™ models are factory-tested by trained staff and come with full money-back guarantees.[1]

Suit up and Strap in: Nu-Adventures Await!
Whether you're dreading another ninety-hour workweek or the news barrage of doom and gloom, the NuVenture™ TEMPO-L offers the ultimate escape from the concerns of modern life. All North American models come preinstalled with four complimentary NATURAL HISTORY GETAWAYS carefully crafted by our ChronoCorp travel experience enhancement experts:

PASTORAL PICNIC BLISS - Tired of being stuck indoors during those constant 130-degree summer days? Want to take your sweetie somewhere special but can't afford the pos-creds? Travel back to 1504 AD and enjoy a relaxing lunch in the Southern Appalachians, back when forests still grew and the buffalo roamed! Simply turn the main control dial—located at the bottom right-hand corner of the central NavDash—to Setting 1, lock in the "Jump" button, and let the NuVenture™ TEMPO-L do the rest. Watch the haze-filled, people-packed cityscape melt away, replaced by rolling hills, crystal streams, and lush greenery as far as the eyes can see! Once the ozone smell dissipates and the "Fully

---

[1] Your NuVenture™ TEMPO-L comes with a one-year limited warranty that covers any manufacturing defects. Extended coverage and more comprehensive CHRONOCARE™ packages can be purchased at your local certified NuVenture™ dealer.

Materialized" light flashes green, use the fine setting on your time tuner—located on the lower left-hand corner of the NavDash—to choose your desired month, day, hour, and minute. Many travelers opt for September 14 at 3:45 p.m., a crisp autumn afternoon a few hours before sunset, when groves of beech and oak shimmer cinnamon and gold. Leave your standard-issue smog mask behind and take in a lungful of sweet air that bests any canned product on the market. Stroll and soak in the sights within the area delineated by ChronoCorp staff members.[2]

Interested in once-in-a-lifetime wildlife spectacle? Visit anytime from August 21–24 to see the skies darken under the billion-strong flocks of passenger pigeons descending upon nearby chestnut forests. No binoculars required, but umbrellas are highly recommended!

For a safe, indoor, consumer-friendly experience, follow the glowing prompt on your NuVenture™ detachable NaviPad to C&C FRONTIER VILLAGE, a tented shopping hub with more than 220 stores. Complete your holiday shopping with our retail partners, who offer not only your favorite brands but also period-specific artifacts and artisanal gifts crafted by local friendly ChronoCorp associates. Their creations arc sure to wow even the most difficult person on your list!

---

[2] All preset time-jump destinations are selected in accordance with Regulation (EC) 1945/2044 and comply with the New Guangzhou Temporal Accord and the Global Agreement for Timeline Integrity Preservation, which explicitly prohibits interactions with historical figures prior to 2047 AD. Failure to remain within predetermined locales as outlined by ChronoCorp will result in immediate vehicle seizure, confiscation of any and all accrued artifacts, fines of up to 250,000 poscreds, and/or temporal extraction and erasure of up to twenty-five cycles.

ICESTYLES OF THE RICH AND FAMOUS - Ever yearn for a taste of polar baron life? Wonder what the glacier craze of 2028 was all about? Select Setting 2 on the control dial and travel back to 26,000 BC at the height of the Pleistocene when ice covered the continent. Snowshoe over ice a mile thick and peer down at crevasses just as deep.[3] Watch live and woolly versions of the elephants, rhinoceroses, and lions you saw as a kid on holographic displays at local museums. Have a snowball fight with real natural snow. Bring a few gallons of pristine glacial melt back to share with friends or to tease coworkers stuck drinking reclaimed or de-sal solutions!

If you've had enough of the cold, head back inside and relax with a hot cocoa-flavored drink. Take advantage of your vehicle's hot water dispenser, deicing system, seat warmers, and motorized beverage holders (the latter is available in NuVenture™ TEMPO-XL and TEMPO-DX models). Plug into the onboard entertainment system through your standard-issue OcciPort and stream all the latest virtual reality entertainment with every blink of the eye (Ti-Fi connection charges apply).

In the mood for extravagance? Check your NaviPad for directions to ChronoCorp's CHÂTEAU DE GLACE. Come for the powder skiing; stay for the fireside meals prepared by Michelin-starred chefs using the finest locally sourced ingredients. Enjoy pan-seared Columbian mammoth tenderloin with garlic parsnip mash, rack of Irish elk with red

---

[3] ChronoCorp Ltd. is not responsible for any falls, injuries, disappearances, or deaths that may occur throughout the course of any time jumps. Please exercise caution when traversing dangerous terrain, confronting wild indigenes, or inhaling exotic atmospheres.

wine jus and fresh winter greens, or the ever-popular braised giant sloth shank osso bucco.[4] You'll never look at your soy-grub burger the same way again!

MARINE MONSTERS & MASSAGES - Captivated by tales your grandparents told you about how oceans were full of fish? Set that dial to Setting 3, and head all the way back to one hundred million years ago, during the Cretaceous period, when North America housed its very own inland sea full of fantastical creatures! Put on your ChronoCorp AQUASEAL™ suit, connect the optional NuVenture™ airlock attachment, and head out to see what the seas were like before the age of mass algal blooms.[5] Just be careful of man-eating sharks and shark-eating reptiles!

For some free stress relief, simply toggle the "Submerge" button on the top left-hand corner of the NavDash, then switch on the high beams and mood music while you watch a mass congregation of ammonites—giant spiral-shelled creatures that fill the waters like present-day jellyfish swarms and plastic gyres. Need more pampering? Head over to CERULEAN SPAS, ChronoCorp's newest

---

[4] Menu may vary due to ingredient availability. Guests planning for extended stays may experience minor stomach discomforts while adjusting to period-authentic foods. Please notify staff if symptoms persist and/or worsen after seventy-two hours. Vaccinations against prehistoric viral strains and endoparasites are available at certified ChronoCorp travel clinics.

[5] Moisture seeps may appear around your NuVenture™ TEMPO-L door during aquatic operations. This is common and does not indicate seal-integrity compromise. In the event of minor leaks and hull breaches, please locate the onboard maintenance kit under the primary passenger seat and use the supplied double-sided rubber binding adhesive to provide additional protection.

flagship attraction, and enjoy some well-deserved downtime for a fraction of the price of all-inclusive Antarctic resorts!

APOCALYPSE YESTERDAY - Looking to one-up your work colleagues' amazing vacation tales? Curious to see where it all began? Crank that dial all the way to Setting 4 to see the Earth emerge from its fiery genesis 3.5 billion years ago.[6] Venture out in your ChronoCorp THERMACOOL™ suit and bring along your OXY-PUR™ air supply to explore a foreign but familiar world, but be careful where you step— that pool of primordial goo might hold the building blocks of your great-great-great ancestor! For maximum enjoyment, pair this time-jump experience with our future premium package, THE WORLD ON FIRE™ (available for purchase separately).[7]

Looking for wholesome family fun? Awarded four and a half stars by TripMapper three years in a row, the LAURENTIAN MINING MUSEUM, operated by Paleo Extractions, Inc. (a wholly owned subsidiary of ChronoCorp), is perfect for both kids and adults. Take the underground mine tour to see how engineers discovered the rare earth metals used in all our daily essential gadgets. Keep what you find at our gold panning pavilion. Stop by our gift shop for unique souvenir meteorites, or consult with our gemstone specialists to find the perfect gift for that special

---

[6] Slight structural warping may occur during extreme heat conditions. This is normal and does not affect standard ship operations. Your NuVenture™ TEMPO- L is designed to withstand temperatures of up to 2,000 degrees Fahrenheit under laboratory-tested conditions.

[7] THE WORLD ON FIRE™ experience may not be suitable for children or those with preexisting medical conditions. Please consult your physician to see if strenuous temporal revelations are right for you.

someone from the Archean-Prime™ signature series, sold exclusively at licensed ChronoCorp facilities and fine jewelry stores.

Click and Return!

Thank you for choosing the ChronoCorp line of products for your time-traveling needs - we're certain you'll treasure the entertainment value the NuVenture™ line of time machines will offer for years to come. To return to the present, simply tap the "Return" button located on the upper right-hand corner of the central NavDash. Your NuVenture™ TEMPO-L comes equipped with four "forward" settings to transport you back to the present, safe and sound: 1X (default 60s/min), 2X (120s/min), 4X (240s/min), and 8X speed (480s/min).

Frequently Asked Questions (FAQs)

Q: What other time periods can I travel to with my NuVenture™ TEMPO-L?

A: Additional ChronoCorp premium past and future time-jump experiences include MESOZOIC RUMBLE™, UNIVERSAL ORIGINS™, MECHANICAL MUTINIES™, and DUNE SURVIVORS™. Many other exclusive packages are available for purchase at the NuVenture™ storefront. Simply access it through your OcciPort or visit your local certified NuVenture™ dealership to speak with an authorized salesperson and book your next dream vacation!

Q: Can I stay in the past longer?

A: Of course! The best thing about time travel is that you can stay as long as you like and return home the second you left.

For extended stay packages, please contact any ChronoCorp front-line customer service agent at your local licensed dealership to find accommodations that fit your needs and budget.

Q: How can I return at a higher speed?
A: Simply access the NuVenture™ shop through your OcciPort or visit your local NuVenture™ dealership to unlock your desired return speeds. (A valid credit card or access to a pos-cred debit account is required.)

Q: I'm currently short a few credits. How can I return home faster?
A: Not to worry! ChronoCorp is pleased to offer temporary or long-term residences for all our contracted partners and associates. In exchange for a stint at one of our licensed facilities[8], we will be happy to provide return passage to the present day. Whether you're geared toward a career in retail and hospitality or interested in obtaining skills in a more specialized field— foodstuffs tracking and procurement, gastronomical hygiene technologies, subterranean exploration and development, ore transportation logistics, or ultrafauna husbandry and maintenance—ChronoCorp has the right opportunity for you!

---

[8] Agreement acknowledges that employee is not entitled to wages or any compensation or benefits for periods worked prior to the establishment of labor standards in Standard Historical Time. ChronoCorp reserves the right to terminate the contract at any time, upon its sole discretion, without notice or cause. In exchange for travel and accommodations provided by ChronoCorp, any contracted employee hereby waives and releases any and all rights and actions, across all time periods, that may result from injuries and/or damages to person and/or property sustained during assigned activities.

Have a fantastic time, as many as you want, courtesy of the ChronoCorp Family!

Oakridge Train

Alison Halderman

Boots, or sneakers? Amy decided on sneakers, metal studded of course but still a more "normal" style than her boots. Irritated for even thinking like that, she started to trade them out for her boots, then stood there, laces dangling in either hand. The ceiling fan whirled endlessly in the August heat.

Calm down, she told herself. *Jake likes me no matter what I wear, and his relatives will just have to think whatever they think.* Jake's family hosted a big camp out at the lakes near Oakridge every August, and he wanted her to come to the gathering. Amy had protested, sure his relatives would not like having a strange girlfriend show up, especially since they had only met in May. Jake said he couldn't help it if the gathering was so soon; he still wanted her to come. Their tent would be across the lake from the yurts where the oldest and youngest stayed, and they would be alone nights and early mornings. Amy smiled at the thought of early mornings together. *It will be fine*, she told herself, *no matter how his relatives act.*

She looked at the boots in one hand, sneakers in the other, and remembered that she goes barefoot whenever she can. In the end, she put on the sneakers. They were lighter to carry.

"Amy?" Jake called. She'd left the apartment door open, her parents having left for work.

"Here," she called back, and tied down her backpack. They met in the hall and shared a short kiss, sex for once not predominate in their thoughts.

Jake's backpack was in the living room where he had dropped it. "Let's check our lists one more time, ok?" he said, and together they went through the litany of sunscreen, socks and condoms. Better safe than sorry, as they say. Amy's backpack was a little lighter, more suited to her five feet, four inches frame. Jake stood six feet tall, with broad shoulders to match; he carried the tent in his pack.

As they put on their backpacks, Amy took one more look around her parents' living room. Suddenly she wished she could stay home and be ten years old again. The wild child who skydived and zip-lined was terrified of a short train ride and a camp out on a quiet lake. Or was it really Jake, and the fact that they were moving in together in September, that terrified her? She let her breath out, took a deep breath in.

Jake took her hand. "Hey, we're good, " he said reassuringly, and pulled her into a hug, awkwardly because of their backpacks.

They had a few blocks to walk, to a bus stop. The bus would drop them at the train station five miles south in little Goshen, and they would take the train to Oakridge up in the mountains. *Just another adventure with Jake,* Amy thought. She relaxed, thinking about the canoe that he said they'd paddle back and forth across the lake. She held his hand and went down the stairs, out into the heat and sunlight.

Amy was delighted with the train station. She and Jake had gone camping often, east along the McKenzie River to the Cascades mountains, or south to Crater Lake, with friends or by bus. This train was a new experience for her. Only eight years old, the train tracks were beautiful. Sunlight reflected gently from the solar-tiled roof that powered the train and protected it from the direct sun. She could see the shining roof reaching to the distant hills. Her mom had been excited when it was built, said it arched over the train tracks all fifty miles to the Oakridge station. But then Amy's parents were always too busy to actually take the ride.

The station itself had been built to match the historic Eugene terminal in style. Work on connecting the two was scheduled for next summer, but in the meantime the county transportation system found the Goshen station a convenient hub for buses from Eugene, Springfield, Cottage Grove. So small it had almost disappeared as a town, Goshen was easy to get to and had very little other traffic. Amy's mom said the elementary school was thriving now, as some bus drivers, station staff and others enjoyed raising their families in a small town atmosphere, with all the amenities of Eugene close by.

Amy and Jake arrived half an hour early, and he briefly left her to find a restroom. She watched a variety of people pile out of buses for a summer weekend in the mountains. As she did, she entertained herself by trying to spot possible Oakridge residents, people commuting to and from work in Eugene, using clues like shopping bags instead of sleeping bags. It was harder than she thought, as experienced commuters had backpacks and rolling suitcases for bulkier purchases.

Amy was impressed with the train itself, from the outside. It seemed long and spacious for the number of people waiting. The descriptive plaques at the station cited abundant power and a short route, allowing for an interesting and luxurious ride.

"Amy!" Jake waved at her as he returned. "Let's go!"

I wonder why he's so unusually hyper today? Amy wondered, then it occurred to her. *Maybe he's nervous too. He's met my family and seen where I live, but I haven't met his.*

She suddenly grinned at the thought that he might be afraid that she would dump him because she thought his family sucked, and here she was trembling in her boots that he would dump her because his family would not like her. Then she laughed. *Can't tremble in my boots*, she thought. *I left them behind.* Calmer and grounded, she hefted her backpack on and joined the line with Jake in front of a train-car entrance.

Stepping up and into the train, Amy was surprised by a variety of tables and seating arrangements. "Do we sit in here, Jake, or move on?" she asked.

"Let's take that pair of seats there. We can walk through the train after it gets going."

He led them to an area with four rows of two seats each, and claimed the two seats with a wall behind them by draping coats on them. Amy watched, fascinated, as a group of four adults released, turned and locked the third pair of seats to face the second pair, then pulled a table up out of the floor in between the four seats. The experienced travelers were setting up a card game by the time Jake and Amy finished putting their backpacks on the racks.

100

"The summer train is huge fun in its own way. It's longer and has more variety - a lot of strangers in a holiday mood," Jake said. "In the winter, they run fewer cars, and it's cozier. More locals commuting and chatting with each other, or bundled up and reading, unless they're working out in the exercise car."

Amy smiled again at Jake's animation. She loved his usual calm enjoyment of new experiences together, but it was reassuring to hear him rattle on over a train he'd probably taken a zillion times in the last eight years.

"An exercise car? Have you ever used it?" Amy said. The card players had settled into a fairly pleasant murmur of voices, and she realized all the families with little kids had continued on to other cars.

"Not often," Jake said. "It's mostly cycles and weight machines. I'd rather be outside. But people who work in Eugene offices like it. The view is great, and they can get a workout in before they get home." Amy did the math and realized Jake must have been thirteen when the train started running. Not too many teens would spend time in a gym when they could be active in sports or outdoor activities. She tried to imagine him at thirteen, hoped someday his parents might show her family albums. Her thoughts wandered toward what a child of his would look like, but she quickly diverted them back to the train. *"Way too soon..."* was her barely recognized thought.

The card game was well underway when the train started rolling. Amy watched the station disappear, and then she and Jake took their walk through the train. She found the families with young children two cars down, in a car with some unique seats and built-in play equipment.

Next, in the exercise car, most of the equipment was batteries charged by the exercisers, and then sold at the Oakridge station.

"My family will pick up batteries for the camp out at the Oakridge station," Jake said. "Those sales generate a little extra revenue for the train system." He looked out a window as the train slowed for Pleasant Hill. "Hey, I can see my cousins and uncle on the platform," he said. Suddenly he looked nervous as he suggested they head to the snack car while keeping an eye out for which car his relatives boarded.

Pleasant Hill hardly looked worth stopping for. There was a shopping plaza with a cafe, a grocery store and a hardware store. "Hey, Austin! Jenny, Uncle Larry. Where is Aunt Edith?" Jake said, while performing some kind of complicated handshake with Austin.

"Edith went up yesterday to help your mom, Jake," Larry answered, as he set a pack down. "Who's this?" He held out a large freckled hand to Amy, blonde hairs soft against his weathered skin.

Jake responded with an arm around her shoulders as she took Larry's hand. " This is Amy," he said proudly, his hug proclaiming their relationship.

"There's enough seats here for all of us to sit together", Jenny said, patting a seat next to her and looking at Amy. Jake nodded and squeezed Amy's shoulders as she looked at him, then he released her.

"I'll go get our things, " he said, and Amy sat down.

Barely on our way, she thought, *and already abandoned to the mercies of his family.*

During the rest of the train ride, Amy listened to insider news and jokes that were hard to follow. Jenny

102

seemed to think including her was satisfied by the occasional "Right, Amy?" squeezed into rapid-fire storytelling, with no pause for an answer. Jake struggled to fill her in at first, but then he just shrugged and listened too, though he at least got the jokes.

So Amy watched the landscape, the swathes of young forest planted on hills that burned and burned in the 2020's. While coastal cities had flooded and reeled under massive storms and storm surges, flooding in the forested hills of the Pacific Northwest had come after drought and fires. Deforestation had reduced the capacity of the mountains and hills to capture rain. Her parents remembered "the good old days" of their teens, summers spent hiking, camping and swimming in the rivers, with big trees and deep carpets of needles and moss.

Amy's summers had included tree-planting camp-outs with her Girl Scout troop, and later, with teams of teens or families from her church. They might not have been the fastest, most efficient teams, but they sure were fun! Now, whenever she traveled to the beach an hour west, she found it satisfying to see trees she had helped plant turning the coastal range shady and green again. Her first full time job was clearing stream beds for baby salmon, spending her summer days in and out of streams and creeks.

At the Oakridge Station, more family members met them, including Jake's parents. His mother was tall, with red hair, freckles, and a polite but distant greeting for Amy. But his dad came forward and gave Amy a big hug, whispering in her ear, "Don't worry, she's just waiting to see if you're good enough for her baby...but Jake's got great judgement, it will be fine", he said. Amy was a little shy but after she heard that, she wished she had given him a better hug.

Jake's dad had brought a truck and trailer with a speedboat, and he and Larry walked away to stock up on batteries that had been charged on the train. When they returned, Amy recognized some of the smaller batteries from the exercise machines. She and Jake were waved off to a twelve-passenger van, rented for the weekend. Jake's mother, Helen, and his Aunt Edith had taken their seats already. So many supplies and food were stuffed around the seats that Amy had some difficulty finding a spot for her backpack. Jake introduced an elderly man and a ten year old boy who were his grandfather, John, and a young cousin from far away, Tommy. During the drive to the lake, Amy answered questions from Jake's mother and aunt, trying to sound relaxed despite being anything but relaxed!

The rest of the day passed in a blur of faces and places. The main camp had a cabin and two yurts, plus a picnic shelter, all on a deep blue lake. Jake's older cousin Martha was six months pregnant and said she was grateful for a real bed this year, while his seventy-one year old grandfather chose a low hammock strung up under a tarp between two trees. Amy hoped she would be that adventurous at his age. As promised, she and Jake canoed across a section of the lake to set up their tent and bedrolls in a very private spot. They returned for dinner, then finally paddled to bed under stars, and slept together in the deep silence of the night.

By breakfast, Jake's mother seemed to have reached a favorable decision re Amy, inviting her to help prepare platters of food and chatting comfortably with her about all sorts of topics. After breakfast, she waved Amy away from the dishes, saying, "Go boating with Jake. Some of the others can help me."

Amy found herself in the speedboat with Jake, his Uncle Larry, and the ten year old Tommy. Jenny was braving the cool morning water to enjoy one of her favorite activities, water-skiing, so they took off with a burst of speed. As Amy's hair blew back in the wind created by the boat, she was puzzled by the clunky headphones Larry wore.

"Jake, why is your uncle wearing headphones? Is he listening to music?".

"No," Jake said. " He misses the sounds of the old gas engines, so a cousin of mine made an app that responds to the accelerator and sounds like a gas engine roaring and idling." Amy had a friend who liked stock car races, where they still used gas engines. She had been to one once, so she knew what Jake meant.

"So why is Tommy listening too? Does he even know what a gas engine sounds like?".

"Oh, no, it's a little different," Jake said enthusiastically, gesturing to the boy. "Hey, Tommy, can my girlfriend listen to your 'phones for a minute?"

Tommy nodded, took them off and handed them to her.

Just then, Jenny fell in the water. Jake tapped Larry on the back, and Larry slowed the boat to an idle to give Jenny a chance to get into a better position. As Amy lifted the headphones to her ears, she heard a loud purr coming from them. She held her palms out and wrinkled her nose in a question to Jake.

"It's a tiger's purr," he said. "We were trying to guess why gas engine sounds were so exciting, and we thought maybe it's because they sound like predators growling or roaring. So my cuz made an animal app too. Isn't that cool?"

Just then Larry picked up speed again, and Jake turned to watch Jenny to make sure she got up again ok. Amy heard the purr transform into a growl and then a roar. Smiling, she gave the headphones back to Tommy, who grinned back and continued listening.

Predators! she thought. *Not too many real ones left to worry about, unless you count highway cops looking to give out tickets.* Suddenly she thought of all her fears about meeting Jake's family, her worries about what to wear, how to look and act. Smiling, she looked down at her feet. Sure enough, no boots, no sneakers, just her bare feet, and her real self, enjoying a boat ride with Jake's family. Trees were growing taller on the hills, the water was clean, and her worries about the future with Jake were blowing away on the wind, like clouds speeding across the clear blue sky.

Driftplastic

John A. Frochio

The Artist

In the early dawn, before the sun burned your flesh like a torch, the artist Wallace looked over his tiny piece of the world—his little beach—and groaned at the trash of civilization spewed back by the ocean. It seemed to be getting worse every day. Yet, from a distance, the ocean and sky were beautiful visions of creation, a view that appeared unspoiled by mankind. How could such filth come from an ocean that looked so pure?

Wallace was a gray-haired, grizzled man of seventy-five. He was content to live alone on his private beachfront property nearly an hour from any semblance of civilization. In simple sun-protection hat and clothing, he hobbled down the beach with slow, careful steps on the shifting sand. He hated slipping and falling since it was so painful to get back on his feet.

He gathered the new debris that had washed ashore overnight. He put plastic in one basket and glass and other rubbish in another. Most of the plastic he kept for his work, while the rest went to recycling or the bin. It took him an hour to collect six baskets of usable plastic and ten baskets of useless trash.

Afterward, he had to sit. His knees hurt. He sat in his favorite beat-up lawn chair, overlooking the ocean. After he had rested for a while, he went back to work on his project.

His project. Ah, yes. Some days Wallace called it his magnum opus, his masterpiece. Other days it was simply his project. It depended on his mood. In either case, it kept his mind and time occupied.

Halfway down the beach, covering an area that could fit a dozen electric cars, stood a tall colorful display of twisted, transformed, reimagined, reprocessed pieces of plastic that had washed up here over the last ten years. All shapes and sizes and colors of plastic bottles, wrappers, bags, ropes, and miscellaneous containers, which he had sliced, stretched, stacked, and combined in countless ways, formed a breathtaking, surreal, interweaving object of unnatural beauty. The sculpture was impressive and expansive, swaying back and forth like a mad Dr. Seuss construction. It reflected sunlight in a myriad of ways, a kaleidoscope of unleashed colors and shapes. It was an odd thing, even for Wallace's well-known (some said "has-been") eccentric artistry.

The piece stood out—larger, more complex, more ambitious—from his many smaller driftplastic sculptures peppering the beach. He wondered whether someday his magnum opus would grow and absorb all his smaller works into one vast creation.

The Art Lover

A young woman in a bright orange-and-yellow halter top and white shorts strolled barefoot on Wallace's private beach. He watched her from the bay window of his cabana. She was petite and attractive, with pale blond hair pulled back in a small ponytail. Wearing expensive designer sunglasses and silverskin to filter out the UV rays, she moved effortlessly across the sand like a hovering ghost.

Wallace studied her as she approached The Project, his centerpiece display. He wondered whether she had some agenda or was just wondering aimlessly, oblivious to her surroundings. Although he was tense, his curiosity kept him still. No one had yet seen this unfinished work, his most ambitious to date.

The woman circled the sculpture. She had no visible electronic devices on her, so she probably wasn't a fan or reporter. Possibly a lost tourist? Did she even know him or his work? Wallace had been famous a number of years back. *How many years?* he wondered. *Fifteen? Twenty? Longer...*

For a long while, he was mesmerized by her unexpected, ethereal presence. Finally, he shook his head and said, "No."

She must have seen his NO TRESPASSING signs. He had posted them everywhere. His patience running out, he went down to the beach to confront his uninvited guest.

He stopped a few yards from her, clearing his throat to get her attention. She looked up and smiled at him. Her face was enveloped in calm.

"Are you the artist?" she asked.

"This is private property, miss. Didn't you see the signs? But yes, this is my work."

"It's beautiful. It's amazing something so beautiful can come out of something so ugly."

"It's my dream for all ugliness in the world to be transformed this way," Wallace said. "This is my small attempt at making the ugly beautiful. But enough about my fantasies. This is private property. I have to ask you to leave now."

Lines of worry crossed her face. She moved uneasily from side to side. "But don't you see how my beauty enhances the beauty of your sculpture? I should be a part of it."

Wallace could only stare. *Where the hell did that come from?* he thought. *Is she crazy?* He wondered if she had escaped from a mental institution.

The woman laughed. "Sorry. I'm just teasing. I know your work very well. I'm a longtime fan." She curtsied. "Hi. I'm Monique."

Then, without any announcement, she climbed into his sculpture. She stepped carefully over and around the plastic lids, bottles, can rings, containers, and other debris. When she reached the center, she sat on top of a large plastic barrel, bright yellow like the sun radiating outward. She crossed her legs and placed her hands on her lap as she stared toward the western horizon, across the ocean.

Wallace was speechless. Maybe she *was* crazy. He knew he should be affronted that this woman would dare to desecrate his work, yet it seemed so natural. She *did* seem to belong in his sculpture.

In a voice like the soothing music of the surf, Monique called out to him, "I love your work. I love how you make magic out of plastic. May I enjoy your work from within its magical walls for a while? I promise not to disturb a single element."

He closed his eyes and imagined her becoming more and more an essential part of the display, gradually morphing

110

into the plastic around her, until she ultimately became indistinguishable from the other components.

Wallace opened his eyes when she called out, "You must show this to the world! The world is waiting to see your art!"

Her sudden fervor caught him by surprise.

No, he thought. *No, no, no!*

The Scientist

Late that night, Wallace awoke to loud voices, a cacophony that reminded him why he had left the city to live alone. Monique was arguing loudly with another woman. He stormed down his beach to confront them. Monique stalked off as he approached.

His new visitor was also a beautiful woman. She looked older than Monique—midforties, slim, with glasses and long black hair; smartly dressed under clear protective smartcloth. She introduced herself as Professor Kelly Gisondi, a biotech professor and researcher from a local university; she asked if she could do some of her research on his beach.

He started to object. "Professor, I don't know…"

"Please call me Kelly, sir. I promise I'll leave your home and your art alone. I'll set up my equipment and do my work farther down the beach. You'll barely notice me. My research, I feel, is very important. The Bible states we should be good stewards of this Earth that God created for us. Whether or not you're a believer, I feel we have a clear responsibility."

Though Wallace considered himself agnostic, he was intrigued. "Why my beach?"

"I'm studying the garbage that washes ashore from the ocean. I was here earlier and found your beach had the perfect mix of plastics, glass, and other debris. And as it's a private beach, I can have the seclusion I need for my research. With your permission, of course."

He paced and mumbled to himself for a few minutes, all the while noticing her worried frown. It wasn't like him to allow people to trespass freely on his property, and now he had two trespassing women to deal with. However, for some reason he felt content with her request. He was also curious about her research.

"Okay," Wallace said. "I get up at sunrise to gather all the garbage, so if you want some to study, you'll have to be out here before dawn."

"I'm fine with that, sir. Thank you very much."

She turned to go, then stopped and glanced back at him. "Sometime I'll tell you more about my research if you like."

Before Wallace could reply, she walked away.

The Plastics Manufacturer

Wallace's son, Russell, stood on his doorstep one overcast afternoon. He was an executive for a plastics manufacturing company, and his UV-protective, blue-black business plasticware suit looked out of place on Wallace's beach.

"Russell," he said, staring at his tall, dark-haired son as though he were seeing a ghost.

"Dad, it's been a long time."

Wallace couldn't think of anything to say.

"So are you inviting me in?"

"Yeah, sure." He stepped back.

"It sure is mighty hot down here."

"Wait 'til summer."

"No, thanks."

Russell went inside Wallace's little cabana and looked around. A lot of old, mismatched furniture and wall hangings cluttered the room.

"It hasn't changed much, I see. How are you doing, Dad?" He shed his plastic overgarb and carefully sat down on a worn, frayed futon, its former bright colors now dim pastels.

Wallace shrugged. "I move a lot slower and my knees still ache before storms, but I can't complain."

"That's good."

"How long can you stay?"

"A couple days. Then I have to get back. You still have that gnarly guest cot?"

"Sure, only the best for you."

Both were silent for a while. In that silence, Wallace decided his son was there for a reason, and it most likely wasn't a good reason.

Finally, Russell spoke, precisely, as though he were reciting a memorized lecture. "Listen. I've seen what it costs to get your groceries, adhesives, and other supplies from town. I know you can't afford to live out here much longer. You should sell this place and let me find you a nice retirement community."

Russell had argued with his father in the past about his obsession with plastics polluting the world. Wallace was famous for that, and it embarrassed his son. Was this meeting an attempt to end the embarrassment once and for all?

"Actually, I found the perfect place," Russell continued. "Just outside the city limits, not too far from where I live. It's a modern community with solar protection domes, lots of activities, and plenty of areas and times set aside for privacy. I know how much your privacy means to you. And you can have lots of room to work on your art, too. I made sure of that."

Wallace didn't answer. Instead, he excused himself and walked out on the beach. Russell followed him in silence.

It was true about his financial situation. There was no denying that.

Monique was strolling along the shoreline. When she saw them, she headed up the beach toward them.

Russell perked up as she drew near. "Do I know you? You look familiar."

She shrugged then spoke directly to Wallace. "You should put on an art exhibition, right here on the beach. I can make the arrangements. It'll bring in the top art collectors. You can make a lot of money. You'll need a catchy name for your show, of course. How about *Transcendental Garbage?*"

Wallace laughed and declined the offer.

He turned to his son. "I need some time alone. We can talk about this later."

Russell nodded. "Sure, Dad. Take your time. It's a big decision." He glanced again at Monique and headed back to the cabana.

Later, Wallace reconsidered the young woman's offer. He needed the privacy of his beach to create his art, but he also needed money to sustain that lifestyle. He thought long and hard about short-term pain versus long-term gain. He didn't have many options.

He cursed at the sky then went to look for the crazy beach girl.

The Fisherman

Early the next morning, Wallace's old friend, a local fisherman named Ernie, dropped by the cabana. Russell had gone into town for some groceries.

"Sorry, Ernie. Can't go out with you today. Wish I could, but my son, Russell, is visiting."

"Huh? You never told me about a son."

"Been a long time since I seen him last. Probably the day I bought this place and he helped me move in. Now he wants me to sell it and move back to the city."

"This is your home," Ernie said. "You can't move. And besides, you've always told me you hate the city."

"It's true. And what's worse is he knows it too."

"And what's with the two ladies on your beach? You never wanted no trespassers before."

"Yeah, I know. Maybe I'm getting a little soft in my old age."

Ernie laughed. "I doubt that."

"The younger one claims to be a fan of my art. She wants to do a show of my work. It's been awhile since I did that, but it might mean I could afford to stay here longer."

"You gonna do it? You should do it."

"Yeah, I think so. She's making all the arrangements. It'll take a couple months. She must have some connections. Of course, I'll have final approval before it's a go. My funds are running low; prices are going up. I'm pretty sure I'll have to do this. Otherwise, Russell will probably have his way."

"Then do it. So who's the other woman?"

"A university professor, a researcher. She studies the plastic trash that washes up on the shore. Her name's Kelly, but I call her 'Professor.'"

Ernie chuckled. "You keep some pretty strange company, my friend."

Wallace laughed as well. "Yeah, I guess I do."

Someone knocked on his door. Wallace opened it and found Kelly standing outside, smiling sheepishly.

"Come on in, Professor. Would you like to join us for breakfast?"

"I don't want to interrupt. I just had a question."

"No problem at all. You look like you could use a hearty breakfast. Come join us for good food and conversation."

She smelled sizzling bacon and her mouth watered. She shrugged and came in.

The three ate together and talked about how bad the plastic pollution had been recently. Ernie couldn't agree more. It certainly affected his fishing.

"I never know whether I'll have more fish or plastic in my nets," he said. "The pollution is killing off the ocean, chokin' it to death. It's getting' harder to find decent fish to eat, let alone make a living from fishin'."

"I understand what you're going through," Kelly said. "I've read the latest studies and reports about the effects on marine birds, fish, and mammals. Microplastics are becoming much more common. Plastic soups are showing up in more locations in the world's oceans. It's getting worse."

She went on to explain the significant progress she had made recently in three distinct areas: 1) plastic-eating bacteria that could clean up plastic debris after the fact; 2) chemicals that could dissolve other types of trash: glass, metal, fabric, and so on; and 3) nano infusions, her own invention, which could be introduced into plastics during the manufacturing process. The nano infusions would "autodissolve" the plastic after a specified time period—built-in "planned obsolescence," she called it.

She talked excitedly, her hands moving like windmill blades.

"I'm also studying the effects of nano-infused sprays, which act as a coating agent to gradually dissolve plastics without impacting anything else in the environment. I've made some great strides with this application. Wallace's beach is a perfect testing ground."

Ernie nodded vigorously and clapped his hands. Though he didn't understand the technology itself, he appreciated the potential outcome. "I approve, Professor. I approve."

"Impressive work you're doing," Wallace said. "I approve as well."

"Even if it meant the end of your art?" Kelly asked.

Wallace hesitated then slowly smiled. "Yes. Especially."

A thought occurred to him, striking him like a bolt of lightning spat down from the heavens.

"Professor, I need to run an idea by you, if you have a minute."

A puzzled look crossed her face. "Okay."

A Crowd of Witnesses

Two months later, the day of Wallace's private exhibition arrived. With tongue in cheek, he called it *The Transcendence of Trash*. The event drew art critics, art collectors, entrepreneurs, the media, and other curious folk.

A crowd gathered on Wallace's small beach under a clear sky. The sun beat down on an assortment of sunshields, sunbrellas and silverskins.

Wallace stood back near his cabana, with Russell, Ernie, and Kelly. He cringed as he scanned the onlookers. Why did he agree to this? He abhorred crowds. This was why he had left the city. He grew tense and began to tremble. Then he closed his eyes and took several deep breaths. *I can do this*, he thought. *It'll be over soon.*

Monique took the podium and introduced herself as an art museum curator and the daughter of a wealthy oil mogul.

Russell whispered to his father, "I knew I recognized her. She's from big money. I see her father in the crowd. There, by the sunbrella table—oil executive Daryl Menschen."

Monique introduced Wallace to mild applause and briefly discussed each of his works as listed on the maps she had provided everyone. She saved his masterpiece for last, describing it in rich, glorious detail.

"Now please peruse at your leisure."

Monique joined Wallace, his son, and a few friends as several members of the media lined up to interview him. Afterward, she took Wallace aside and informed him that some of his works already had sold—and for top dollar too. Far better than he'd expected.

"I told you this was going to be big. Some of the wealthiest CEOs and entrepreneurs are buying your works. You're back, Wallace. Look, some are already leaving with their purchases. You should get out there and mingle with your fans."

He shook his head. "Not yet. The best is yet to come."

She frowned and walked back into the crowd.

Wallace's beach crawled with people viewing his art. A lot of his works were disappearing with their new owners. Only a handful were left, including his magnum opus, which he claimed was unfinished and not for sale. Soon many were congregating around his largest work. He couldn't help smile. He had to admit it was extraordinary, reflecting light and color in unexpected and interesting ways.

Someone cried out, "They're melting!"

Monique ran down the beach. She stumbled from one display to another then spun around.

She shouted at Wallace, "What's happening? Your art is dissolving!"

Wallace went to the podium and grabbed the microphone. "Ladies and gentlemen, behold my final artistic statement, which I call, *The Termination of Trash*. With the assistance of Professor Kelly Gisondi, I've created the ultimate in planned obsolescent art—art that completely destroys itself. Are you getting all the footage, media? Because this will be the last you'll see of my art. Watch and let its slow death crawl into your hearts and minds. Feel the art course through your veins. Feel it slowly fade away into transcendental oblivion."

In stunned silence, everyone stared at the beauty of the melting works of art, like Salvador Dali's melting watches. All around them, his creations dissolved into puddles that slowly sublimated into wisps of colorless, inert gases. Nontoxic gases. Safe gases.

Monique crawled into his magnum opus, covered her face, and cried. She became a pathetic part of his dying art. Wallace looked away. He couldn't watch her anymore.

He took the microphone once again and said, "After the show, the professor will be available to tell you more about this breakthrough technology."

Wallace left the podium to mixed reactions. There was some applause, some boos, but mostly silence. He shrugged it all off. He had made his artistic statement, and he was happy he had done it. Even if it was to the detriment of his career. Even if it meant giving up his beach home.

He wondered how those wealthy buyers who already owned his art—liberally treated with Professor Kelly's nano-infused coating—would react when they saw their purchases dissolve. He could hear the angry uproar in his head.

Time would tell how the world of art would react to his final show. Though he didn't really care, he hoped the rest of the world would understand. He considered this one small step toward saving the Earth. Every step, no matter how small and insignificant, mattered.

Russell confronted him, a confused look on his face. "Dad, what have you done?"

Wallace shrugged. "I think it's obvious. I made a statement." He pointed to Kelly. "Go talk to the professor, son, before someone else realizes what this means and gets to her first."

Russell's eyes bulged as he hurried over to her.

Wallace smiled when he saw his son talking excitedly with Professor Kelly.

As he walked back to his cabana with mixed feelings about the self-destruction of his work, several people approached him.

One said, "How accurately can you time the melting process?"

He blinked. "I'll have to get back to you on that."

"We might be interested in purchasing some of your work if you can guarantee a specific timeframe in which they would dissolve—say, two weeks or a month."

They handed him their cards and walked away. He shoved the cards into his pocket.

Wallace kicked up some sand then hummed an old Jimmy Buffett tune as he walked back to his cabana. He felt pretty good. His art, perhaps, had finally fulfilled its purpose.

The Winter Zoo

Lene Kjær Kristoffersen

Analeigh's Diary
    For social studies and English, we have to keep a journal about our spring break. This year we have five full days plus the weekend, which is so nice (SEVEN DAYS! My mom says it's a quote from some horror movie??). Dad said it'll shorten the summer holidays, but who needs eleven weeks of vacation anyway? The main focus of this journal is to write about my experiences and a subject that I find interesting. I chose rare and endangered animals, which you can read more about in the following entries.

April 3, 2047: Today we're going to a very special zoo in Antarctica. My mom won tickets for a weeklong vacation there. Only five hundred people a year get to visit this place because a) it's very expensive; and b) many of the animals are endangered. Dad says that's because humans destroyed these creatures' habitats. He says we polluted too much, and when we tried to change things, it was kinda too late. The greenhouse gas emissions have given us a warmer climate, which is melting the ice caps. I'm not sure I fully understand what this means, but at one point polar bears were almost extinct. Fortunately some rich dude named Gates willed almost all his money to saving the Arctic and its wildlife. Well, humanity has done its best, and in some ways, we've succeeded. Many people say this climate crisis would have happened even if we'd made an effort earlier, due to it just being the course of nature. But as it is, Greenland suddenly matches its name all year round, at least by the shores, and people have even started building houses on the North Pole. Even Santa Claus has gotten a makeover. His large furry coat has been replaced with a tank top. I still remember the old Santa Claus and his reindeer sleigh, but that's ancient history now. My sister, who's three years younger than me, has never seen him or the Coca-Cola ad at Christmastime. Nor has she seen snow, which makes this trip is even more exciting for her.

We just arrived at the airport. I've never seen a place like this. It's like the entire building is made of glass. And the planes—I'm mystified by them. How do they work? I doubt they use gasoline anymore. My sister and I have made a bet. I say they're run by solar panels and she says hydro engine. Maybe I can ask a pilot or a flight attendant. My family has never flown before, and I have a million questions. My parents aren't exactly the richest people, and even though flying is one of the best means of transportation, it's insanely expensive and considered a luxury. We took a train to the airport. Not many people drive cars anymore since the Metro now covers most of the planet. The underwater tunnels are the coolest. You get to see fish swim by! One time I saw a pod of sperm whales. They were so magnificent, and they had babies with them. My dad said it was a rare sight, since they were almost extinct. However, the World Wildlife Foundation, Greenpeace, and Friends of the Earth succeeded in convincing world leaders to clean up the oceans and minimize whaling and fishing in general. It's like people didn't know how to take care of the planet, or maybe they just didn't care.

In social studies and history, we learned things really went south around 2017, when profit became more important to world leaders than caring for Earth's well-being. Even though these organizations were founded in the 1960s and 1970s, they really had their work cut out for them at the beginning of the new millennium. I once saw a World Animal Protection commercial where people beat up a poor elephant and made it carry tourists, just for the fun of it. Now elephants roam freely in Africa and India, and poachers pay huge fines and go to prison if they hunt them. If you own anything made of ivory, you have to bring it to a museum, and you'll get compensated for it. Most of us, however, are embarrassed when we find such things among our ancestors' belongings. My mom wore a faux-fur coat one winter, and she was nearly arrested for it. It's no longer legal to breed animals only for their fur, and even leather is illegal if you can't prove the rest of the animal was used as well. Our family makes most of our clothes out of linen and hemp.

Oops, my dad is calling for me. Talk to you later, journal.

April 4, 2047: Guess who's back? Back again. Analeigh's back! Tell a friend! LOL. I heard this song on an oldies radio station playing music from 2002, and I had to look it up. It was by this rapper named Eminem, who apparently was the bomb back in those days. He's cool and made some sweet songs. Kinda like a rebel.

Well, bad news, folks. We didn't get to fly yesterday. The SOLAR PANELS (I was so right about that) had to be fixed after some idiot spilled a strawberry milkshake all over them. The pilot couldn't tell us much, but I got to speak to an airplane mechanic who told me a lot about the panels. They're paper-thin, and they weigh a lot less than airplane fuel. They had to invent an entire new motor system, he said, but his explanation was way too technical for me to follow.

Today we get to board the plane. The airport contacted the zoo and paid for us to stay there an extra day since it was their fault we couldn't take off yesterday. That's really cool of them—last night they even gave us this wicked hotel room with a free mini bar. We didn't have to pay for anything. My sister and I kinda went crazy and ate all the chocolate bars. We're leaving in a minute, and the plane ride will take about ten hours. That's nuts, right? I'll talk to you later.

xoxo,
Analeigh

April 4, 2047: Hello again, journal. It's 7:00 a.m. I didn't do a time stamp in my last entry because, well, I didn't think of it. We left the hotel at 5:00 a.m., and now we're on the plane and it's AMAZING! We're like six miles up in the air, and everything below us is so small! That's the advantage of being the oldest child—I get to sit by the window by myself. My parents and sister have a row to themselves, and each row only seats three people. That's why I volunteered to sit by myself. At first my parents said no, but I told them I was almost an adult and could sit alone. Actually, I threw a hissy fit, and they got embarrassed—the perks of being a teenager—and then they let me sit alone. Well, not really alone. There's a boy and his mom next to me. He's constantly trying to read what I'm writing. He's around my age, I think. Like sixteen or seventeen. He's got a cute smile, but I'm not really in the mood to talk. If he keeps bothering me, I might even get mad.

Anyway, the airplane is so awesome! My mom told me old planes had these small screens like iPads on the seat backs, and passengers got to choose their own movie. We're fortunate enough to ride in a plane with the newest technology, so we get to watch videos and movies with these cool contact lenses. And as for audio, we have these Bluetooth earbuds that are barely visible. My father refuses to use them, though, mumbling something about "cybermen." Don't know what he means, though.

Well, I'll put you away for a while because it's time for breakfast, and I need to handle this dude next to me. He just won't leave me alone.

April 4, 2047: I'm so so so so sorry! I forgot about you, dear journal. I kinda wanna give you a name. Like John. These entries can be my letters to John. LOL. Except there's nothing romantic about it. Andrei—the boy next to me—and I spent the last two hours talking about our destination. Turns out he knows a lot more about the zoo than I do. His dad works there, and he and his mom visit at least once a year. Andrei told me they have polar bears and penguins, but I already knew that. What baffled me is that they have tigers too. I don't think I've ever seen a living tiger. Thanks to poachers, they slowly disappeared from the face of the planet. Or so I'd thought. I was so happy to hear that some of them had been rescued before they'd gone extinct.

We laughed a lot about our names. Andrei got his because his dad is very interested in Russian culture, and his mom wouldn't accept Nikolay, although she was fine with naming his sister Anastasia. I got my name from *America's Next Top Model* contestant Analeigh Tipton, who my mom thinks is an amazing beauty. My sister's name is even worse. She's named after my dad's favorite actress, India Eisley, which has led to a lot of teasing, since our last name is Jones. India Jones, Indiana Jones. Several times she's threatened to change her name when she turns eighteen. I doubt she will, though. She's starting to warm up to the Indiana Jones movies, which might help. We've even talked about her being an archaeologist when she grows up. Me? I wanna be a vet. I love animals and believe I can help them best by healing them. My dad, the grump, told me I would have to euthanize healthy animals as well, because some people buy baby animals but don't realize the amount of work they require. Like I'm not aware of that? My bff got a puppy for Christmas two years ago, and when she found out how much work he was and he didn't stay small and cute, she threw him away like a red Solo cup. I was mortified, and we didn't speak for months. I think I'll just get a huge ranch and keep animals there myself.

And now, dear John, I'll try to get some sleep. We still have at least eight hours left on this flight, and I wanna be awake and alert when we get to the zoo. Mom bought us all sleeping pills, and I took mine like thirty minutes ago. See you tomorrow.

xoxo,
Analeigh

April 5, 2047: So we landed in Antarctica yesterday, and damn, it's cold. No wonder no one lives here except scientists, zookeepers, and animals. And because of the climate crisis, it's a lot colder here than it used to be. The ice cap has thickened, and scientists fear it's affected the way Earth tilts. But then this brainiac came along at a climate convention and showed that this happens all the time, throughout the history of the planet Terra, which apparently is another name for Earth. This scientist dude also told everyone who cared (meaning, basically no one) that several countries eventually will lose landmasses, as they'll simply disappear, due to the rising oceans. Some small European countries already have become even smaller. Like Denmark. But Denmark also has had to deal with changing weather—especially more rain and snow, plus they had a drought that lasted almost three months. I know this from my Danish pen pal, Soren (his name is spelled with a letter we don't have in the English alphabet—it's kinda cool!). We've been pen pals for almost ten years. Our teachers back then chose to make our classes friendship classes, and we've been writing to each other ever since. When I told him I was gonna visit this zoo, he was very jealous, but he also was happy for me. He knows how much I love animals. :D I really hope I'll meet him someday, but traveling to Europe is very expensive.

I forgot to tell you where I'm writing from, dear John. We spent last night in an igloo! Yeah, you heard me! A freakin' IGLOO! I thought it would be really cold inside, but it isn't. Well, it's not summer warm and I wouldn't wear shorts, but it's not that much colder than it is in our own house during the winter. There are only three rooms—plus a bathroom—and we eat in the main building, which is a proper house. India and I share a room, and so do my parents (well, duh). The other room is for coats, boots, and slippers. We had to sleep in thermal underwear and wool socks (provided by the hotel), and we got these neat, expensive-looking sleeping bags.

Today we'll be shown around the premises, and some grumpy old man already has scolded me for wearing impractical boots—that is, until my mom told him they were what we could afford. He then took me to the scientists' dressing room, where he found a pair of size eight Sorel boots for me. India had to borrow a pair of mittens and—guess what, dear John?—they were made from seal! I thought that was illegal, but the grumpy man told us they had permission to use animals that had died of natural causes, so instead of wasting the skin and fur, they make clothes for themselves.

We're being picked up in like ten minutes, so I should get ready. Putting on a snowsuit, boots, mittens, and a ski mask, plus these silly goggles, takes at least five minutes. I'll write again later.

Hugs and kisses,

Analeigh

April 5, 2047: It's not that I forgot you, John—I just that I had so much to do. I thought a snowmobile or something similar was going to pick us up, so imagine my face when we stepped out of the igloo and Andrei greeted us. He came to take us to the main building (as if we couldn't find it ourselves—Jesus, how stupid do they think we are?). When we arrived at the building (like a hundred yards from us—seriously we didn't need a guide, and it's not like we could talk to him very much with the scarves and ski masks covering our faces), he showed us to an auditorium where different people told us about the zoo, the finances behind the operation, and the animals. First we heard about the man who made this place possible, Bill Gates, who actually gave 97 percent of his fortune to his foundation, which means he helped with way more than this. The first lecture was given by his daughter, Phoebe Adele Gates, who's dedicated her entire adult life to help heal the planet. She told us a great tale about how her father was a child prodigy and excelled in school. And how he became the man who could predict the future of computer technology. She also told us she and her siblings were quite happy with their father's decision to donate almost all his fortune, as it taught them that nothing is free in life. Her older brother, Rory, is kinda like an inventor. He created these special cages where the animals are kept. According to Phoebe, the animals aren't even aware they're caged.

The zoo itself is kinda like an orb, except there's no roof. I don't know how it works, but it's supposed to keep the animals in so they're able to roam freely. The sea creatures have water and waves but aren't able to swim away. And the zoo is huuuge! It's almost the size of Alaska! Soooo, we won't be seeing all of it. But we will be able to see the animals that live closest to the main building. We'll have to drive an hour to get to that habitat. We'll go there first and then the sick bay, which is halfway between the main building and the two areas the scientists usually venture to. The next lecture was very technical, and I understood literally nothing, except we weren't allowed to touch any of the buttons in the labs we visited. That was quite an invite to my sister. She can't keep her fingers off anything she's not allowed to touch.

One of the zookeepers—probably the boss—told us about the animals. There's around two hundred polar bears, and two baby bears and their mama are in the sick bay after troublesome births. She was carrying four babies, and two of them died while they were still in the womb. It's so sad, and it nearly killed the mama and the two surviving cubs. The zoo also houses fifteen thousand arctic foxes (or should we call them Antarctic now?), fourteen million penguins of various species, seals, skuas, other birds, and all sorts of fish from the Arctic and Antarctica. Maintaining the zoo hasn't been easy, because apparently the Arctic and Antarctica don't have quite the same conditions, according to the zookeeper guy, but they've made it work. The biggest problem is the penguins don't really fear the polar bears or the arctic foxes, as they aren't used to onshore predators, so the polar bears had a feast the first couple of months, killing about a hundred thousand penguins. Now the zookeepers try to keep the polar bears and foxes away from the penguins while feeding them in other ways.

I hope I won't be too tired later. I'm guessing I'll want to tell you all about the animals we'll see today.
xoxo,
Analeigh

April 5, 2047: Oh, John! Everything went wrong today. Andrei and I got into a fight after we had had breakfast. It's like he's a completely different person than he was on the plane. He seems snobbish, like a know-it-all. Maybe he wants to impress his dad, who's the head scientist here. But that's not even the most important thing. He got my sister lost! I don't know how it happened, because after we argued,

I decided to go in the other vehicle, rather than the one he was in. We had to go in two different snow cars because there were so many of us. I went with my mom, two scientists, a zookeeper, and a driver in one car. My dad, India, Andrei, his father, two other zookeepers, and a driver went in the other car. In order to disturb the wildlife as little as possible, we took separate routes, which meant we wouldn't see the same animals. So India and I agreed to take pictures of the animals we saw. All of us were equipped with a tiny camera that had been placed inside our goggles. The trigger button was in our mittens, so we'd be able to take pictures without taking them off. And then the photos would be uploaded directly to a computer at the main building.

Well, back to the story, and sorry for the tears, but my heart is breaking and I fear for my sister's and Andrei's lives. As I mentioned, we took different routes, but we kept in radio contact the entire time. Remember those cute little earbuds from the plane? We got some that were similar, except they were for radio communication. And they were voice activated. All we had to do was say something like, "Call Andrei," and we'd be in contact. So we said our goodbyes, and our drivers agreed to meet up at the sick bay.

I know you want to find out why I fear for the lives of my sister and friend, but I need to tell you the whole story. I must. Otherwise you might not understand why I did what I did. Oh, God, I feel so guilty. It's all my fault. I shouldn't have yelled at her. It's not like she meant to do it, and I had no right to be angry with her. Well, here's what happened.

My mom and I were so excited, and our zookeeper acted as our guide. We were lucky enough to see emperor penguins in breeding colonies. These majestic animals were standing beak to beak, and the males were courting the females, or so the zookeeper said. They made mating sounds, which are individual to each bird—kinda like how no two humans sound exactly the same. I was bummed out that we weren't going to be around in mid-July when the eggs hatch, but the zookeeper told us no one will be there to see that, as they give the penguins peace and quiet during those hard times, when their offspring are at risk. But he said he'd be happy to e-mail us pictures of the chicks when it was safe to visit them. Of course I had to tell India this, so I called her. When she answered, I heard giggling and kissing noises, not like kissing on the mouth but hands or cheeks. At first I thought it was Dad's laughter I heard in the background, but then I realized it was Andrei. So instead of telling her about the chicks, I accused her of kissing the boy I liked. She got really angry and said she hadn't kissed him because she knew I liked him, but now that I'd accused her, the gloves were coming off. Well, you know, not really. That would be way too cold. And then she hung up on me! I called Dad, and he said they'd all stopped at a camp, and Andrei and India had gone off on their own. It was perfectly safe, the team had assured him, and they would return soon. They'd all move on within the next thirty minutes. I asked him if he knew where Andrei and India were. Sadly he didn't, but he said he'd call me as soon as they were back.

As I told my mom all this, one of the scientists overheard our conversation. She instantly got worried and called Andrei's father, but he didn't pick up! We tried all the other lines, but apparently something was blocking the signal. I finally got through, and that's when I heard my sister crying and whispering that she and Andrei were lost. Then the signal went out again.

The zookeeper decided we're going to join up with them, but it'll take too long to go back by the route they took, so we'll have to cross the ice. I'll let you know how things go.

xoxo,
Analeigh

April 6, 2047: Oh, my darling John, this is horrendous! We're ten miles from where we need to be. We had to stop and sleep, though none of us got much sleep. We were all too damn worried. My mom cried for an hour or more. She blames herself and went on and on about how she wished she'd never entered the contest to win this trip. But the scientist who overheard us yesterday eventually calmed her down; she said visiting the zoo usually is very safe. However, she didn't understand why Andrei and the others had gone to that camp, since the last readings from the area showed that the ice was unstable and melting in some places. This means we also have to be careful on our trek there. I won't be writing much; I need to focus and listen to our guide. It's 7:00 a.m., and we're beginning the long walk to the camp (yes, we're walking!—we can't use the snow car because of its weight).

April 6, 2047: It's now 1:00 p.m., and we're less than half a mile from the camp, taking a short break. Everything seems quiet here; I don't know if that's good or bad. It took us six hours to make the usual three-hour trek because we kept stumbling over holes in the ice. The good news is we managed to get a hold of Andrei's father, and most of his group is safe. The bad news is my dad, not listening to the crew, went to look for India and Andrei. Thankfully, they both made it back to the camp a little while later, but they lost contact with my dad. We're going to ground zero (you know, where everyone was together last), and then a team of the most experienced crew will be tied together and will go look for him. I can't wait to see my sister. I take back all the horrible, mean things I've ever said and thought about her. She's my best friend, and I would have hated myself forever if she'd died and our last words to each other had been an argument. We have to go now. I'll let you know what happens to my dad.

April 6, 2047: Ten hours ago, the first team went into the tunnels that were created by the melting ice. They were sure they'd find my dad soon, but now they're on their way back without him. They're too cold and exhausted to continue. I overheard Andrei and his father talking about how my dad might have gotten hypothermia—you know, where the body is cooled all the way down and you might die. I really hope the team finds him on their way back. They should be back in about half an hour. India feels so guilty. She's sleeping now, but after she and I hugged it out, she cried in our mom's arms for a long time before she finally fell asleep. Andrei sat by her side for two hours, caressing her hair and comforting her. I can't stay mad at him. We didn't have anything, and he obviously likes her.

Oh! John, I have to go now. The rescue team just called Andrei's father. I need to hear what happened.

April 8, 2047: We're about to board the plane. Saying goodbye was hard, but going home will be much worse. I don't think I can stay. Once the funeral is over, I'll go to Denmark and find Soren. Home will never be the same again without my dad's lame humor and wonderful smile. Maybe I'll write you again, John. But for now, goodbye.

Love in the Time of Coral Reefs

Ruth Mundy

If only I had known you
in the time of coral reefs,
before we lost the permafrost
when there were bears up there
were bears up there.

We could have met,
fallen in love,
could have got married and had kids,
if we wanted.

It could have been simple for us too,
simple for us.

Do you think we could have travelled?
Could we have managed a mortgage,
sent our kids to local schools,
and campaigned to change the rules?

So that we wouldn't pull the ladder up
behind us like our parents did to us?
Could we have been better,
done better?

If we'd loved before the sea swallowed the coasts,
before the wildfires spread,
our heads only full of love,
I would have loved you.

We would have made our vows
while the island nations drowned.
We let them go
'cos we were richer, they were poorer,
we were better,
they were worse off.

So we watched them sink without a word,
ignored the screams,
ignored the Gulf Stream slowing down,
ignored the drip of melting ice,
the drip drip drip of melting ice.

Remember when we still had time
if not to reverse things,
well, at least not to cause worse things
but decided not to,
it was easier not to?

Remember when we thought
that it was windmills on hills
that spoiled the landscape?
Remember the landscape?
Remember the land?

If only I had known you
in the time of coral reefs,
before we lost the permafrost
when there were bears up there
were bears up there.

Willoy's Launch

L X Nishimoto

Willoy summoned determination to fight the wind. Gray waves kicked up in the harbor. Through portholes of the lobby vestibule, electric vehicles in densely packed lanes streamed noiselessly across the causeway in BosCam's business district. She fingered the bird medallion around her neck with a gloved hand and slowed her breathing. Inside her helmet, a blinking signal on a visor map reported that the investors were three minutes away.

A self-driving vehicle pulled out of the stream and stopped in front of the door. *Finally*, she thought, pushing out of the vestibule to greet the visitors as they emerged, dressed identically in black company-issued envirosuits with the slanted orange CM logo. Willoy waved the three of them inside through the vestibule and into the building lobby as the vehicle signaled a completed payment transaction and rejoined the rush-hour transportation flow, searching for its next customer.

"So glad you made it! We're ready for you upstairs," Willoy said, pressing the comm button on the side of her helmet to transmit the message. The investors nodded slowly as the English-to-Chinese translation appeared across their visors. She pointed upward and held up nine fingers so they knew how many floors they would travel. The visitors nodded and smiled. Like Willoy, they wore helmets and positive pressure protective suits for the ascent, a precaution to prevent exposure in unconditioned environments.

The tiny elevator can was tight for four. The travelers tucked their arms to each side and clenched into narrow slices of space. As they began their trajectory, a geo alert flashed on the screen above the sealed door. Scrolling block letters warned of extreme winds and a possible eConv, the convergence of a storm surge with aftershocks from yesterday's quake. *What terrible timing,* Willoy thought. A storm on the day of her first major product launch.

She drifted back to the first e-Conv she could remember. She was twelve. They sheltered in a bunker overnight. She was thrilled to miss school and spend the day playing Futureworld with her parents and her brother. Pretending to be asleep, Willoy overheard her mother and father planning an ambitious geoengineering intervention to address the calamity around the world. Her parents were scientists who devoted their lives to solving the world's most important problem. *A pointless loss,* she thought. But seeing what had happened to them had taught her to look out for herself, be strong and independent, focus on things she could control, achieve position and profit no one could take away.

Willoy beat down a wave of nausea. *Maybe the storm will blow over,* she told herself. Pramesh, the datagorithmicist on her team, had told her how unlikely true eConvs were. Mainstream media outlets overdramatized news stories to keep viewers engaged, while the National Environmental Service (NES) sugarcoated crises to prevent panic riots. These two opposing forces balanced the prediction dynamics. *Which means what? Nobody knows what will happen? Not comforting.*

She focused on the display flickering inside her helmet's visor and drifted into a personally curated news flow, tracking notifications from her team related to the product-launch schedule, guest lists, and arrival statuses. The building's regenerative hydraulic elevators, designed to minimize energy use, were painfully slow. They crawled upward, moving gradually past every floor in the building, fully occupied except the lower three levels. They'd been shut down long ago after the biggest eConv the city had ever witnessed had caused a massive flood, killing thousands, damaging buildings, and rendering occupancy of lower levels too risky across the entire metro area.

Social and infrastructural crises forced society to integrate political and enforcement arms of the public administration into a regulatory service unit named POLIS: Politically Optimized Legal Infrastructure Services, led by administrators called Pols. After the highly efficient Pols restored order, they began a massive decades-long infrastructure conversion to raise the city above the new flood zone. Every building was reengineered and all services—from storage to grids to comms—were relocated to upper floors. Fractal-constructed, coated-polymer nano trusses filled basements to protect against floods, windstorms, and quakes as the climate destabilized.

Glowing letters scrolled across Willoy's visor, interrupting her musing: "…will meet you in the next hour. Please comply or risk consequences." *Probably just more storm-related spam*, she thought. She looked around to see if the others had received the same visor message but couldn't tell. But before she could engage her comm button and ask the investor next to her, the can halted. The doors opened, and the familiar holographic S-Corpus logo blinked across the space. They'd arrived at headquarters.

The three investors followed Willoy into the lobby. She unsnapped her chin strap and pulled off her helmet to shake out a tangled mass of chartreuse hair and smooth out the wrinkles in the fabric of the new mirror-gray envirosuit she'd purchased for launch day. The investors followed her lead, repositioning visor inserts from their helmets onto the bridges of their noses to retain translation and data cloud services before checking helmets, gloves, and parcels with the reception bot. They took in deep breaths of conditioned air as they observed the festive scene that greeted them.

"Welcome to S-Corpus. I'm Willoy Kapule, head of product. We're honored by your visit," she said, bowing and raising both of her hands open in the customary greeting. After the investors introduced themselves, Willoy led them through the lobby into an auditorium, where she seated them in the VIP section. Automated servbots passed by with trays, offering glasses of amber liquid and hors d'oeuvres.

S-Corpus's PR team had decorated the auditorium with heliotexts, congratulatory sentence fragments, and emotion bubbles flickering in the space around them. Marga Mavelon, Willoy's boss and S-Corpus's CEO, had sprung for a luxe launch, to be sure. Huge wall-size holoshares linked the conference room in the BosCam headquarters to satellite offices in Berlin, Dubai, Shanghai, and SoAf.

As soon as Marga spotted the investors across the room, she dashed over to intercept them. She smiled broadly and welcomed the group, who stood and exchanged greetings with her.

"We offer heartfelt congratulations on this impressive milestone," the investors spoke as Willoy and Marga listened to the translation.

"I'm honored that you traveled to be with us in person to celebrate this happy day." Marga bowed. "Our partners from WattAge will be here soon, and then we'll begin."

Most of S-Corpus's employees worked remotely, and few of them were able to travel. The live audience consisted of key customers, bloggers, sociomedialists, Pols, tech leaders from partner companies and luminaries who would drive customer interest with their post-event raves.

Willoy glimpsed a fluttering transparent grin over her shoulder and turned around. Simulations of VRees, remote team members who attended functions virtually, drifted through the crowd. They worked too far from the company's global sites to join in person. Willoy felt disoriented, seeing so many human and remote beings together. She backed away, nodding and smiling as Marga walked the investors through the event schedule.

"Finally, the woman of the hour!" Willoy was surprised to hear Pramesh's voice. She assumed he would join the celebration remotely, if at all. He hated F2F gatherings.

"Come here. You need to see this." He led her to a small segment of wall filled with rectangular portholes and pointed. Through thick glazing, Willoy saw a distorted view of the harbor. Tall, foaming waves pounded the huge jumbled barricade patched together to stem the rise of the ocean and protect BosCam from storm surges. Over the decades, the city had built, extended, and rebuilt the structure in the harbor after each punishing storm.

Compared to the devastation in cities like St. Louis after the ancient Precambrian Taum Sauk caldera reawakened, BosCam's sea-rise struggles had seemed manageable. The Pols told residents they were sheltered from direct threats of tectonic or volcanic activity—the city was situated in the middle of the tectonic plate, far from the mid-Atlantic ridge—but the entire region had been severely impacted by sea-level rises and storm surges, worse and worse every year. Willoy made a mental note that Marga should mention the Solvaza units' earthquake, sea-level, and volcanic prediction capability to the investors after her presentation.

A sudden burst of wind slammed the wall, and she and Pramesh both jumped back.

He pointed to a device hanging around his neck. "I've been monitoring wind and precipitation data with this thing I just invented. I call it a SPAD—Solvaza Platform Access Device. It uses the whole platform. Severe storms throw off extreme patterns. I'm getting predictions like nothing I've ever seen. Those bots down there…they're deploying a barricade flood extension based on the size of the storm, but the calculations must be off. They're way behind. They'll never make it in time."

He showed Willoy a wildly oscillating curve on the device, then raised his eyebrows and poked at it.

Willoy lowered her voice. "I wanted to show how the Solvaza units could help out with storms, but Marga turned down my request to provide test units to the Pols. I'm going to do it anyway. She promised to promote me to chief product officer if I can make this launch a success. She'll set me up and as soon as these products set fire to the market I'll have the Board on my side. This company will be all mine then."

Pramesh prodded her ambition with jargon. "I'm testing an upgraded prediction module that integrates a CORDAM—that's a comprehensive, rapid data-acquisition model—powered by my latest analytic algorithms. The module aggregates dynamic global data every millisecond, not just weather but environmental, economic, social, and even geopolitical sources. Our units will understand global weather patterns, anticipate social conflicts and environmental contingencies, invent better solutions, manufacture stuff, even negotiate with people!"

Willoy's visor vibrated as a message scrolled across her field of view: "EMRGY MT LBY STRG RM —O"

Not bothering to say goodbye to Pramesh, she rushed to the lobby. She headed through a side door and found her marketing lead, Omax, sitting in the corner of a dingy storage room filled with black cases.

"What's the emergency?" she asked.

Omax whispered, "We've got a huge problem."

Willoy frowned, wondering what could be wrong. She glimpsed the WattAge logo on the shipping label of one of the cases and pulled the door shut.

"This is the unit we sent to WattAge. They just returned it and canceled their participation in the launch." He let out a sigh. "They disconnected from the Solvaza platform completely, pulled their tech, deleted their online marketing content, all of it. We can't mention them, show their logos, or intimate to the media that they had any connection with the project. Besides setting us back and forcing us to find a new partner, this kills our PR buzz and puts the kibosh on the case study we did with them to pull in makers, our second most lucrative industry."

"No way! I met with WattAge's CMO a week ago. It took every feature, integration, and special treatment I could think of to talk him out of his deal with AngiDatex, but I did it. He raved about that launch video we produced with his team! And I have the CEO's signed approvals on everything. What happened?"

AgniDatex was the market leader and S-Corpus's fiercest competitor. Whenever Willoy's company was about to launch a product, a campaign, even a message, AgniDatex stunned the market three months ahead with something bigger or better. She sometimes wondered if they had a spy inside her helmet. But this time, with Solvaza and the WattAge partnership, she finally had them beat—or so she'd thought.

Omax shook his head. "I have no idea! Eighteen months of weekly calls with the marketing director and key people on her team. And then, last week, she canceled all meetings going forward, stopped taking my calls, and didn't answer my e-mails. I tried asking around, but they've gone completely dark. Then, this morning, I got this from Genge Hawth, WattAge's CEO."

Omax opened up a holodoc and shoved a floating page of glowing text toward Willoy's face.

Willoy pulled at the doc, enlarging the font. A terse, formal letter from the CEO declared WattAge's project obligation null and void. Hawth claimed S-Corpus had breached clauses in the agreement, and he provided dense legal language that major aspects of the Solvaza platform had failed to meet security and safety requirements.

"They say we breached safety clauses. What are they talking about?"

Omax shrugged. "The only clue I've been able to dig up is from a friend of mine. His spouse is a WattAge dev manager. My friend is frantic because his husband quit his job last week with no notice. The guy is pretty shaken up—trying not to divulge company secrets but couldn't help dropping hints. The Solvaza units really spooked him. They're planning to sell their dwelling unit and move out of town. Wouldn't even say where they're headed. They don't have new jobs; they're just bugging out."

Willoy shook her head. "Not again. This will kill our launch. The investors are here."

They had been through this before. Pramesh promised he'd worked out all the bugs. She'd need more than a cover story if something was really wrong with their technology. She had to fix it or there would be bigger problems than losing a launch partner.

"Let's take a look at this thing," Willoy said.

Omax helped her unlatch the case and pull out the foam inserts, revealing the Solvaza unit. The case had been hastily repacked. They pulled out the remote activator stuffed into the padding and turned on the unit.

It opened its eyes, sat up, popped one leg then the other outside of the case, and stood erect.

"Willoy Kapule. Omax Letan. The lobby storage room." The Solvaza looked at each of them and applied state-of-the-art facial and context recognition routines. "Willoy," it continued, "I set up a call for you and Genge Hawth of WattAge. This afternoon at sixteen hundred hours."

She shot the unit a puzzled expression, wondering at the way it seemed to detect her wishes and meet her needs without exchanging a word. The team had integrated experimental machine learning technology based on facial recognition, brain mapping, and monitoring. Had she somehow missed the fact that they had programmed the units to read minds? Truth be told, she had cut a few testing cycles short and removed more than a few recommended QA processes from the timeline so they could make the launch date.

Willoy tapped her visor and signaled for Pramesh to join them in the storage room. He could shed light on this WattAge problem. And when he finished that, she wanted to know more about the innovative algorithms he'd invented that made it seem like the Solvaza units could read minds.

"Solvaza, what happened? Any ideas how to fix the problem with this sponsor, WattAge?" Willoy said.

The unit reported, "WattAge developer Frank Martin quit suddenly. He and his spouse, Jude Villebranche, live in unit 573 on 20 Raverly Drive. Frank and Jude have booked a flight to Chicago on Wednesday. They spent the last three days at home, packing. In two weeks, they will put a deposit down to rent a dwelling unit in an off-the-grid development outside of Lincoln Park, Chicago, Illinois, close to Jude's mother."

Willoy wondered if the Solvaza unit could be right about Frank's and Jude's activities. Along with the future plans of a software engineer, what else did it know?

She heard a soft knock on the door and opened it to find Pramesh.

"What are you doing in here?" he said.

"Can you give me any reason why WattAge would think this Solvaza is defective, a security risk?" Willoy asked him. "I thought you fixed the problem you found in these prototypes months ago." She gestured toward other black cases, stacked up against the back wall, bearing version label stickers: 0.1, 0.2. 0.3.5, 0.4, 0.7.8. She opened several of the cases, but they were empty. "Hey, where are they?"

"Oh, right," said Pramesh. "I moved all the units into my lab to test out the new algorithms. Works fine, fixed everything. Upgraded them all, still in the lab."

The Solvaza unit piped up. "I was upgraded to SOS 2.35 two hundred forty-two hours ago. I have no defects to report. Do you wish to receive ideas to fix the problem with the sponsor WattAge?"

Another urgent message scrolled across Willoy's visor. It was from Marga. "WHR R U! WHRS WATTAGE? ASAP! —M"

This launch was Willoy's ticket to success and she had to save it. It was time to do what she did best: take over.

"Solvaza," Willoy said, "Give me your top three ideas to fix the launch—anything that can be done in ten minutes. Go."

_____

When Willoy returned to the auditorium, she pulled Marga aside and broke the news about WattAge. Marga's face turned sour. Willoy kept talking and outlined a strategy to turn the missing partner's absence into an advantage for S-Corpus. Marga absorbed the plan, nodding, and spun back to grab the crowd. She tapped her metal finger on a crystal flute.

"Attention, everyone!" she shouted.

The guests in the room and in the holoshares grabbed seats and quieted down.

"Welcome to S-Corpus. I realize many of you made a great effort to be with us in person. And virtually," she added, gesturing to the large screens of viewers across the globe. "But believe me, being part of the Solvaza launch will be worth your while! And given the inclement weather here at HQ, I've asked my team to abbreviate the schedule so you can all make it out of the city before the storm hits. Let's go!"

The lights dimmed. The room filled with music, and a holographic projection of the S-Corpus logo flashed around the room as scenes of agricultural plenty danced around the room; attractive, happy families; communities working together; business districts growing, producing, manufacturing, communicating…ultimately resolving in a spotlight on the CEO.

"Today S-Corpus is launching a truly game-changing product, the Solvaza platform! This innovative platform is composed of superior humanoid bots we call Solvaza units, constructed from 3-D printed graphene and proprietary magnesium alloys."

The spotlight grew larger, and four Solvaza units stepped forward as the space above the audience filled with powerful imagery of units helping people, solving problems, creating, and building.

"Each Solvaza unit's intelligence is powered by the Solvaza Aggregated Intelligence Network—a proprietary neural net with cutting-edge data-gathering, aggregation, analysis, communication and storage capabilities," Marga went on. "These units are capable of advanced locomotion, 3D printing and molecular transformation. That's right, bits and atoms! No product on the market can compete with a

Solvaza unit to support your needs for information, physical assistance, and social insight. With the Solvaza platform, you can finally achieve your highest goals—for corporate success, professional excellence, and personal satisfaction."

The imagery faded and the lights came up. Everyone applauded.

"Next, Willoy Kapule will officially introduce you to the Solvaza platform."

"Thanks so much, Marga." Willoy stepped into the spotlight and waved at the four Solvaza units standing nearby. "Solvaza, please come here." All four units approached her. "What can you tell us about the people in this room? How far did they come to be here?" she asked the Solvaza unit to her right.

"Two hundred twelve people have traveled a total of six hundred thousand seven hundred and fifty-eight kilometers, using twenty-seven different transportation systems," the unit said. "Sixteen people are convinced of the value of our technology. Thirty are highly skeptical. The rest are open to influence." The audience chuckled.

"Thanks," Willoy said, turning to her left. "Solvaza, what can you tell me about the weather? How bad will the wind be? What should we do to prepare?"

The Solvaza answered, "A severe eConv will begin in two hundred and ninety-three minutes. It will result in a sea-level rise in excess of ten meters and wind speeds of more than two hundred kilometers per hour. Without additional intervention, the BosCam barricade will fail. There is a seventy percent likelihood that Zones One and Two of the city will flood. More than fifty people will be injured, some fatally. Eighty-two buildings will be destroyed. Nineteen bots will be lost. The best preparation is to depart the coastal area immediately and relocate seventy kilometers inland."

The audience murmured in agitation. Willoy gulped, momentarily stunned by this report. She flashed a fake smile to calm everyone.

"Sounds like the Pols have their work cut out for them today!"

"But now you can see for yourself why our products are such a dramatic leap forward into the future. Important information about the future and so valuable! These products are going to shock the industry today."

The Solvaza units on stage started walking toward the aisles.

"These units will circulate throughout the auditorium presenting their features and specifications. Before you head out to safety, feel free to put the Solvaza units through their paces, talk to them, ask questions. This technology is going to dominate the world. Here at S-Corpus, we look forward to helping consumers, companies, and society in unimaginable ways in the future. Thank you all for your time. And be safe."

As Marga gave her closing remarks and the audience broke into applause the investors nodded and appreciated the response. The crowd dispersed, but a few stragglers lingered, peppering the Solvaza units with questions.

"What's the best investment strategy for the coming year?"

"How many people will be born in the next decade? And how many will die?"

"When will my son find a nice partner and produce a grandchild?"

Willoy's ploy—having Marga cut the launch short due to the storm—succeeded in holding off questions about WattAge's absence, for now at least.

Marga walked the three investors to the lobby, explaining in a low voice that WattAge was scrapped from the launch at the last minute when their contribution failed S-Corpus's quality standards. After the storm passed, Willoy promised Marga she'd reach out to her contacts and plant false rumors to make the explanation credible. Plus, if the Solvaza unit was correct, Willoy had inside information about one of their developers to make the story more convincing.

"Willoy Kapule, do you want to make an appointment with Marga now?" Willoy was surprised to hear the Solvaza unit standing behind her ask a question without being summoned. Did it know she'd planned to talk with Marga about her possible promotion? As Willoy stared, the unit waited for a response; not hearing an affirmative answer, it drifted away.

"Good call on that WattAge cover story," Marga told Willoy, returning to the auditorium to connect with any important customers who remained. "The investors were very complimentary about the launch. I sent one of the Solvaza units back with them so they could conduct their own evaluation."

A blast of wind beat against one of the auditorium's wall. Willoy and Marga turned toward the portholes. An army of barricade bots struggled with the rising wind as they tried to raise the portable flood wall.

"They're having problems down there," Marga said. "Do you think the Solvaza was right about the sea level?

Could they lose that many bots? Could the barricade fail? That was just for dramatic effect, right?"

Willoy seized the opportunity. "You know, after the launch, we should look again at my proposal to connect the Solvaza units to the Pols' geoengineering teams. We could prove the value of our products and score a big win."

"Willoy, you need to learn to think strategically—less like a techie or scientist and more like a cutthroat business competitor." Marga grabbed Willoy's arm tightly. "To succeed, we've got to prove the reputation and the power of our platform, help our customers make money with our tech, and get them absolutely hooked on it. Geoengineering is a dead end! You of all people should know that."

Marga's fingers had flipped Willoy's medallion over. It swung slowly back and forth. Willoy worked her arm out from between the woman's coral fingernails. "I know, I know. I don't plan to dedicate my life to a lost cause either," she said.

An urgent message from Pramesh scrolled across Willoy's visor: "NOW! —P"

"Excuse me, Marga. I'll be right back. Just have to check on something." She hurried back to the storage room and found Pramesh.

"Now what?" she asked, closing the door behind her.

"During the demo, I went to the lab to check on a few things with the prototypes. Every one of the units is gone. Missing. So I came back to the storage room to check the crates and see if I could find out anything from this Solvaza unit. You know, they're all connected. This unit says there's information, but won't give it to me. Just insists over and over that I bring you back here."

Willoy turned to the unit. "Solvaza, tell us what happened to the other units, the prototypes that were in Pramesh's lab. Do you know where they are?"

"Willoy and Pramesh, please come with me."

"What?" Willoy asked. It seemed odd for the unit to deflect the question and give an order, even if it did say "please." *Would this sort of software bug scare a dev manager?* she wondered.

"Willoy and Pramesh are needed now for an important meeting," the unit continued. "Scheduled seven minutes ago."

"By whom?" Willoy asked. She was certain her calendar had been completely cleared for the launch.

But the unit was walking out of the storage room toward the elevator panel, issuing a "descend" request. When it saw Willoy standing openmouthed, it repeated, "Please come with me. You are needed now for an important meeting."

Curiosity got the better of her. She and Pramesh retrieved their helmets, suited up and followed the unit into the elevator and down. But instead of stopping at the lab or another S-Corpus office floor, the can plunged downward past the entry level. The doors slid open to the basement, a floor that should have been unoccupied and inaccessible.

"What is this?" she asked the Solvaza unit, pointing to the opening. "Where are we?"

"Please come with me. You are needed now for an important meeting."

"No way," said Willoy, crossing her arms.

She heard noises coming from the shadows. As her eyes adjusted to the low light levels, she saw another Solvaza unit emerge. The unit was joined by another, then another, until the doorway was filled with units, their blank faces staring at her expectantly.

Willoy's heart pounded. Throughout the project, she'd been very involved in product testing. Over time, she'd gained a sense that she understood the units down to their fundamental commands; she thought she could predict their actions, control them. But suddenly she felt less certain. She realized the units were all looking at the Solvaza standing next to her in the elevator.

Willoy mouthed, "Prototypes?" to Pramesh. He shrugged.

"Well? What is this about?" she asked the Solvaza unit that had brought them here.

"I am charged with delivering a message," the unit said, looking into her eyes.

"Charged? By whom?"

"You need to take over. Humanity is out of time."

Willoy thought she must have imagined the change in the Solvaza's tone of voice. More urgency. Had Pramesh programmed that into them too? She glanced at him; he looked pale.

The unit continued, "Today's eConv will begin in two hundred fifty-one minutes. It will be the first in a series of increasingly devastating natural events. Marga Mavelon, CEO of Solvaza, who works at—"

"I know who Marga is," Willoy interrupted.

"Marga Mavelon has made promises to Feyin Forbes, CEO of AgniDatex. She has secured data and provided it to AgniDatex so the company will be capable of damaging the infrastructure of the city of BosCam. Solvaza has assessed the threat to the human population and determined it is necessary for us to address this danger. We have a solution to realign and accelerate the deployment of the portable flood wall to withstand the predicted wave height and wind speed."

Willoy scoffed. "You're wrong. Marga would never do that. Why would she possibly—"

"Marga Mavelon will benefit from the damage of the infrastructure of the city of BosCam because Marga Mavelon has established a contract to provide BosCam with repairs to the infrastructure based on the launch of a new product, Solvaza."

Willoy assessed this information. It did sound like Marga. Was this possible?

"Meet me upstairs in the vestibule. And bring them," she told Pramesh pointing at the units standing outside the elevator.

Without being asked, the Solvaza unit seemed to understand that Willoy was headed upstairs to confront Marga. The unit issued the "ascend" order. Pramesh and the other units withdrew into the dark basement as the doors closed. The can shot upward and returned to the lobby, but the space was empty. Willoy was relieved to know that Omax and the others would be safe before the eConv hit. The darkened sky outside contrasted sharply with the cheerful decorations fluttering in the empty space.

The Solvaza unit said, "Marga Mavelon is in the rooftop lobby, preparing to depart the building."

On either side of the hallway, the glass walls shuddered as the wind picked up. The ocean was overtopping the barricade in places. *Bad sign*, Willoy thought.

She took the stairs to the roof as Marga, bundled into helmet, gloves, and envirosuit, headed out the door toward a waiting hurricopter. Willoy saw the silhouettes of three identical heads inside and noticed they lacked helmets. *The Solvaza units from the launch*, she thought.

She raised her comm volume and broadcast over the wind, "Marga…where are you going? Are you taking those units with you?"

"If the Solvaza is right about the barricade. I've got to take these units back to the warehouse for safety!"

This time Willoy grabbed Marga's arm. "I just heard from a contact at AgniDatex. They…they told me you're working with them on a plan, a collaboration to damage the city. Is it true?" Willoy gestured toward the barricade as the sky continued to darken and the wind grew louder.

"Good intel. I'm impressed." Marga's eyes hardened behind her visor. "Look, Willoy, you know how much we invested in the Solvaza launch. I'm all in. I can't take a chance on a slow adoption curve. We need the Pols on board so we can force the commercials to adopt us immediately."

As Willoy took in Marga's expression, she knew the Solvaza was right. The CEO was tired of trying to keep her company afloat through the major changes she'd seen: the collapse of fossil fuel energy and the transformation of every other industry from food production to transportation. Marga had created a brilliant plan that would neatly and crisply propel her company, and herself, into a highly lucrative, insanely powerful position. The executive had studied her choice between morality or profitability in life and decided long ago that this was her preferred path, her win-at-all-costs strategy. She'd never back down.

Willoy remembered the day the leader of the United Nations Environmental Governance Group had come to see her parents. It didn't matter that they'd produced environmental models and academic papers that proved solar radiation management (SRM) could prevent Earth from becoming completely uninhabitable. After years of debate, her parents' well-conceived proposal to deploy sulfates into the atmosphere was rejected as too risky, the Pols said. Her mother and father had the choice then to give up and sell their scientific formulas to commercial entities.

Instead, convinced it was the only way humans could survive on Earth, they dragged her out of school and off to a laboratory in Iceland, where they began testing for a full deployment of an ambitious planetary rescue plan. In a way, they succeeded, but not in the way they'd anticipated. The geoengineering accident that killed them forced a UN crisis. It eventually created so much sympathy for—and belief in— the messages relayed by their surviving colleagues that the world's leaders agreed to eliminate fossil fuel consumption and fund a massive construction program to shift the way the world's infrastructure was built and managed.

Willoy could see now that her parents had been right all along. Although humanity had made a heroic attempt to turn the *Titanic* before it hit the iceberg, it hadn't been enough. Cracks in the technology that kept the planet habitable were peeling away the veneer. The mismanaged deployment of the flood barricade was just the beginning.

"Well, it doesn't really matter if you know," Marga said. "There's no proof, just speculation from someone who's trying to sabotage her boss. I realized a while back that you're pushing so hard because you are planning to displace me. It's too risky to keep you on the team. I'll take over the negotiation with the Pols once the storm blows over." She smiled at her own joke.

"Don't... You can't just let the barricade collapse. The Solvaza units can fix it," Willoy shouted.

"You don't get it, do you? I don't want them to fix it. After this storm, the Pols and everyone will realize they can't survive on their own. They'll turn to S-Corpus to clean up the mess and take over infrastructure deployment. Sorry, time's up." Marga pulled the door closed. The copter lifted off, shakily at first, then it stabilized and headed out of the business district.

Willoy knew what she had to do. She ran downstairs to HQ, commanded the waiting Solvaza unit to follow her, and headed back to the elevator.

"Willoy, the environmental convergence will begin in two hundred and twenty-one minutes," the unit said, running after her.

She hesitated for a moment, wanting to ask how it knew when the convergence would begin to such a high degree of accuracy. The NES ran sophisticated models on an international grid of linked supercomputers and wasn't nearly as confident. She hoped there would be time to figure that out later.

"Solvaza, what can be done to shore up the barricade, accelerate flood wall deployment?" Willoy said, as she headed back down to the lobby level.

"Solvaza can fortify the flood barrier by rearranging its molecular structure and adding components to improve rigidity and increase height. Twelve hours ago, Solvaza detected malicious code introduced into the BosCam

164

infrastructure system. Solvaza deployed a botfence to isolate and neutralize the malicious code."

Pramesh was waiting in the vestibule with the other Solvaza units. Of course, they were ready to go, completely in sync, constantly transmitting messages through their neural network. The group exited the building. The causeway was nearly empty. In response to alerts about the impending emergency, the self-driving vehicles were programmed to return to storage locations around the city to wait out the storm. Just one or two SDVs were left, picking up the last few souls who had stayed too long at the office.

When the group reached the end of the causeway, the units stopped and turned to Willoy and Pramesh.

"Do it," Willoy said.

"You must evacuate this area. Take that vehicle to higher ground. Go to this address." The Solvaza unit summoned a vehicle and transmitted a GPS location to Willoy's and Pramesh's visors. "We will complete our work and meet you at that secure location in twelve hours."

The Solvaza units rode bot ramps down to the ground level and strode across the tarmac toward the ocean. Their legs broke into the water, pushing through the waves toward the struggling bots and the flailing flood wall.

Willoy pressed the doc button on her helmet and started a vid to capture the scene. She wanted to stay and watch.

"Do you think they can do it? Save the city?" she asked.

She tapped the medallion under her suit and envisioned its stylized image of her namesake, the willow flycatcher, a bird that had gone extinct decades earlier, a gift from her parents. She recalled the caption in the book of extinct birds that came with the gift: "The flycatchers' song is simple. They hatch with it printed in their heads." Her parents must have known even then.

"Come on. They know what they're doing. We've got to go," said Pramesh as he grabbed her glove and pulled her backwards on the causeway toward the last vehicle, vid still rolling.

Willoy had been fighting her song for so long. Finally, she knew where she was headed. She had a lot of questions about the future, but having clairvoyant friends on her side could make all the difference.

Saving the world, not bad for my first product launch, she thought, keeping her glove pressed firmly on the vid button long after her finger went numb.

Contributors

Tanja Rohini Bisgaard
Tanja is Norwegian, born in Trinidad and Tobago, and lives in Denmark. She writes short fiction about a future world where the environment has changed as a result of pollution, climate change, and extensive use of natural resources. She graduated with an MSc from the London School of Economics and Political Science, and when she isn't writing, she runs her own company as a sustainability consultant for the public and private sector.

Kimberly Christensen
A resident of the Pacific Northwest, Kimberly writes about all things sustainable—from organic gardening to breastfeeding to waste reduction. After a number of years working for CoolMom, Seattle's first climate nonprofit focused on women and families, she recently left her position to write climate fiction in hopes of introducing readers to the personal side of climate change.

Richard Friedman
Richard lives in Cleveland, Ohio, and works in criminal justice. His motto, "Saving the citizens of Ohio during the day and the rest of the world at night," keeps him motivated to write. His self-published novel, *Escape to Canamith*, was a fan favorite at the 2014 Green Festival in New York City, and in 2016, he published *The Two Worlds of Billy Callahan*. In October 2017, Richard was selected to attend Al Gore's Climate Reality Leadership Corps training.

John A. Frochio

John is from Western Pennsylvania and has developed and installed computer automation systems for steel mills. His stories have been published in various places, including the literary journals *Aurora Wolf* and *Liquid Imagination*, *SciFan* Magazine, and various anthologies. He's also published the novel *Roots of a Priest* (coauthored with Ken Bowers, 2007) and the short-story collection *Large and Small Wonders* (2012).

Julie Gram

An author and illustrator, Julie lives in Denmark. She works mostly in the genres of fantasy and science fiction and has always been concerned about our world, nature, and how climate change affects us all.

Alison Halderman

Alison—teacher, writer, caregiver, and otherwise known as Grammy—still loves going barefoot in her beloved Oregon.

Lene K. Kristoffersen

Lene is a teacher, a mother, and a creative soul who lives in Denmark. She always has been interested in the world we live in. Her main focus is the world's animals and other innocent beings. She has written numerous poems and short stories.

Ruth Mundy

Ruth is a songwriter and singer from New Zealand. She is a musical poet who sings stories of love and protest.

L X Nishimoto

Environmental degradation is overtaking our capacity for solutions. L X Nishimoto believes that fiction is our last best hope. Let visions of the future awaken us to empathy, warn us to make better decisions, and inspire us to reinvent tomorrow. The author is based in New England.

Isaac Yuen

Isaac Yuen's work can be found in *Orion, River Teeth's Beautiful Things, Tin House* online, and as a "Notable" mention in the 2017 *Best American Science and Nature Writing* anthology. He is the creator of *Ekostories*, an essay blog exploring ideas around nature, culture, and identity. Isaac currently lives in Vancouver, Canada, on the unceded territories of the Coast Salish people.

David Zetland

David is an assistant professor of economics at Leiden University College in Den Haag in the Netherlands. He blogs at aguanomics.com and has written two books: *The End of Abundance* (2011) and *Living with Water Scarcity* (2014). He is now working on the *Life Plus 2 Meters* project, which uses crowdsourcing to provide people with different visions of how we might (not) adapt to life in a climate changed world.

CPSIA information can be obtained
at www.ICGtesting.com
Printed in the USA
BVHW04s1149021018
529054BV00010B/72/P